Jennifer Oddy
Islington April 89

UNUSUAL BEHAVIOUR

The police receive an anonymous letter informing them that "something strange" is going on at Hollycroft, a large, decaying Victorian house in a London suburb. At the time, the police are making a house-to-house search in the neighbourhood, for IRA bombs and bombers. So Chief Detective Inspector Corby, and his brightest CID recruit, Mary Copthorse, put Hollycroft high on their list of priorities. But they find nothing to arouse their suspicions.

The house, and its neighbour Greenways, have been bought by a small-time developer, who has temporarily let the rooms at Hollycroft at low rents to a motley collection of people. Next door, at Greenways, there are squatters, and on the other side of Hollycroft there's a convent where Sister Catherine is less than happy. Even the police have their own personal problems: Corby's marriage shows signs of cracking, and his wife is at odds with their daughter, while Mary's boyfriend grows increasingly resentful of her job and her refusal to say she will marry him.

Here are intriguing human cross-currents. Lives make unlikely conjunctions; and why is the mysterious Mervyn digging a secret pit in a hidden corner of the Hollycroft garden? Gradually, the parts cohere, and surprising truths emerge. Lettice Cooper brings instinctive sympathy to a wide range of characters, and provides her policemen with some intriguing puzzles.

UNUSUAL BEHAVIOUR

A NOVEL

by

LETTICE COOPER

LONDON
VICTOR GOLLANCZ LTD
1986

First published in Great Britain 1986
by Victor Gollancz Ltd,
14 Henrietta Street, London WC2E 8QJ

British Library Cataloguing in Publication Data
Cooper, Lettice
 Unusual behaviour.
 I. Title
 823'.912[F]   PR6005.O4977

 ISBN 0-575-03862-4

Photoset and printed in Great Britain by
WBC Print Ltd, Bristol

Dedicated
with affection and gratitude
to
Natasha and David
in whose house most of this book was written

NOTE

During the house-to-house search for IRA bomb makers and bomb materials in 1981, the Police issued a notice asking members of the public to report "*any unusual behaviour*".

L.C.

PART ONE

1

"COME IN."

Chief Detective Inspector Corby pushed away from him the two piles of typescript, reports read and unread. He sat back in his chair, flexed his arms, and took off his reading glasses, horrid things which after he had worn them for a year still annoyed him. There was far too much paper work involved in this house-to-house search round London for IRA bombs and bomb-makers. Corby felt like crowning the next person who talked about needles in haystacks, but that was what it was. Still so far as he could see there was no other way of doing it.

Now that his attention was withdrawn from the reports, he saw the heavy rain sluicing down the window, and heard above the constant bourdon of traffic from the street, the ringing of telephone bells in the other rooms.

"Sit down, Mary. It was East Walburn again this afternoon, wasn't it? I suppose you didn't find anything?"

"Not a sign."

The young woman who plumped into the chair opposite him looked wet but rosy and cheerful. She had pulled a soaked scarf off her head, but had not yet shaken out the two wings of light brown hair that lay like pressed fern leaves against her cheeks. The shoulders and sleeves of her dark blue anorak were black with rain water.

"Better take that thing off hadn't you?"

"Nothing gets through it," but she ran down the zip and slipped out of the coat. Certainly nothing had touched the very clean white sweater underneath it. She was, Corby

9

reflected, one of the few women who looked nearly as smart when they came out of uniform as they had looked wearing it. Her promotion to the CID was only three months old. She still radiated her pride and pleasure in it. Corby, an old friend of her father's, who had suggested the police as a career for her, was pleased with her and with his own perspicacity.

"People in East Walburn, some of them, do keep the most extraordinary things in their out-houses and garages but we didn't find anything that could be used for bomb-making."

"Who went with you?"

"Sergeant Byeford and PC Williams."

"There are a lot of Irish there."

"Yes, there's a colony round the Catholic Church. Some of them lodgers, but most of them residents who've been there for years. Could be 'sleepers' of course, but we didn't find anything to suggest it."

"Did you get as far as a street called Robin Hill?"

"No, we shan't get to that before the end of next week I should think. I know Robin Hill though from when I was on the beat."

He smiled; she sounded as though that had been such a long time ago.

"It's on the far side of the children's playground. Between that and the Answold Housing Estate. Robin Hill's a run-down middle-class patch: three biggish houses standing back from the road in their own gardens, with a strip of wood between the gardens and the housing estate."

"There's a letter here from someone about a house on Robin Hill. Called Hollycroft Grange. Do you know it?"

"Yes. It's the middle one of the three houses. The one above it on the slope is a convent. I think there are or were squatters in Greenways, the third one below Hollycroft. Hollycroft was empty when I first came here but I heard lately that a developer had bought that and Greenways, and was converting them into expensive flats. I don't know how far he's got with them."

10

"There's a letter here about Hollycroft. Anonymous. It's odd how many people feel it's safer to be mixed up with the IRA than with the police. Have a look. Its been fingerprinted, a blank . . . and photocopied. Posted in WC1."

While she read it his mind slipped away for a minute to problems at home. It had so far seemed to his wife, Lucy, and to him that their elder daughter, Jessica, was the difficult one. As soon as she had turned into her teens she had reacted violently against everything from the law of the land to her mother's excellent cooking. She played pop music too long and too loud, she flounced in and out of the house as if it was an insult to her dignity to be obliged to live in it. But now, having got a place at Leeds University, and gone there six weeks ago with the farewell remark that she would come back at once if she didn't like it, she was writing cheerful and even affectionate letters. It was her younger sister, Matilda, who had turned sour, and he wished he didn't feel as if Lucy was mishandling her. He had admired the unruffled way in which she had dealt with Jessica, but she seemed to feel a personal resentment against Tilly; there was an edge of sadism, almost . . . Tilly had always been his pet. Now she was making trouble between her parents. He found himself wishing that he could have a holiday away from them all, but even if he could seriously contemplate doing anything so unprecedented, he couldn't take any leave now while the bomb hunt was on.

Mary Copthorne looked up from the paper.

"It's just like some of the other letters we've had, isn't it? She . . . it is she?"

"I think so."

"Well she thinks that something strange is going on at Hollycroft, but she doesn't want to get anyone into trouble. I wonder what she thinks is the good of writing, then? But she says the police did ask people to report any unusual behaviour that they noticed, so she feels it her duty. It would be more help if she said what the unusual behaviour is.

"She wants to keep out of it. Or she wants to get someone

11

into trouble without their knowing that she did it. Is it worth while bothering about it until we come to Robin Hill?"

"Yes, I think it is. Come here and have a look at the map."

He picked up a ruler from his desk and swivelled his chair round. Mary came over to look at the large-scale map of their district which hung on the wall behind him.

"There's Robin Hill. You say that Hollycroft is about halfway up?"

"Yes. There."

"Well, opposite it, across the children's playground, is North Road, and Alston Street turns into North Road. It was in Alston Street that Clinton found the shop where a young man with an Irish accent had bought half a dozen wristwatches at once just before the last bout of postal bombing started.

"Now look at the other side of Robin Hill. Garforth Street running through the new Council Housing Estate, and into Cheriton Street at the top of the hill. The Three Feathers is in Cheriton Street. It was outside that pub, do you remember, that someone noticed the Cortina two nights before it was used for the Fulham bomb."

"Oh, yes, I remember."

"In my view any hint from that area between Alston Street and Cheriton Street is worth a quick follow-up.

Go and have a look at Hollycroft and the other house tomorrow afternoon. If I can manage it I'll come with you. I'm getting stupefied with paper work. I'd like to do an hour or two outside. Thank you, Mary. Goodnight."

2

AT THE END of the afternoon Robert Prentice came out of the office of the North London Electric Appliances Company where he worked, and started to walk back to his lodging along the rush-hour crowded pavement.

At one crossing the street lights had failed. The line of cars became a queue, which finally stopped altogether. The drivers at the back sounded their horns; those in front scowled at this irritating waste of energy. A policeman stepped into the middle of the road to sort out the tangle; in a minute or two the line of cars moved easily forward again.

I suppose, Robert thought, if I did that she'd think more of me. Specially if I was in uniform.

For two and a half years now he had been waiting for Mary Copthorne to get tired of being a police-woman, but lately, especially since her promotion to the CID he had been conscious of an uneasy suspicion that she might be more likely to get tired of him.

They still slept together in her tiny flat once or twice a week. When they began it had been heaven. Now it was still lovely but also something he really felt grudged to him. When they woke in the morning she was so briskly ready to get off to work. She made his coffee and toast and then turned him out. He could tell that her mind was already moving forward to the police Station, and her colleagues there. He privately thought police work unsuitable for a woman. He wanted her to give it up and marry him. If you didn't want the thing to be permanent you were in his opinion only playing at loving. It was time to have a serious talk with her.

He lodged in a turning off the High Street with a Pakistani family who kept a newspaper, sweet and tobacco shop. The idea had appalled him when he was first looking for rooms, he had meant only to stay there for a week or two until he found something else. But it was comfortable and he had come to like them very much, they were so kind.

He took off his business suit, and did a few exercises. He was careful to keep fit. He looked in the mirror, and approved what he saw. He was fair, clear-skinned and blue-eyed. He put on a comfortable woollen sweater knitted for him last Christmas by Mary's mother, who had moved, if reluctantly, with the times. He ran downstairs; the two younger Paki

13

children were waiting for a game of which they never tired. They ran to the front door and held hands across it chanting, "You can't go out," and giggled with delight, when he said, "Oh, you little horrors!" and removed them one at a time so that the other one could slip back: He had had enough before they had, and walked out past them.

Mary had only just come in. She was still in her working clothes; the parcel of food she had bought lay wrapped on the table, but she greeted Robert with her pretty smile, and as he hugged her and felt the springiness of her breast, and smelled her own personal smell, his grievances for the time being melted away. She was his girl and that was it.

"I'm late. You heard about the Bank Raid?"

"No. What?"

"It was the London and Northern Bank in the High Street. This morning a few minutes after twelve. There were three of them, one with a gun. The old cashier there, Robinson, tried to get to the emergency bell. They cracked him on the head, and he's had to have a dozen stitches. He's in hospital with concussion. There was a pregnant woman in there cashing a cheque. She collapsed, and she's threatened with a miscarriage. Tom Byeford was the first of us to get there, they shot at him but luckily missed. The thieves got away with quite a lot of money! We haven't caught them yet."

With a desire to reduce her excitement he sketched a yawn.

"Happens to every bank nowadays, doesn't it? It's routine."

"It's the first time it's happened here. Nothing's routine when it's on your own patch."

She had begun to unwrap the parcel.

"There's some soup in the fridge, real soup that I made yesterday, and I bought two chops. There are some cooked potatoes we can fry up and a cake we can have with our coffee okay?"

It was perfectly o.k. but he did not want to say so. He fancied that she had taken the minimum of trouble.

14

"Could you lay the table while I slip into something easy?"

She felt that he was not happy, and looked at him with closer attention.

"What sort of day have you had?"

"Oh much as usual: we don't run to high drama in my job."

"We have a lot of dull days, too."

She came back in a pair of old jeans and a loose jersey. Her cheeks were bright from being hastily dashed with cold water.

"Now we won't be long."

She lit the grill and pushed the two chops underneath. She began to stir the soup.

"Would you get two soup bowls out?"

"Shouldn't they be warmed first?"

"I always think that if you pour very hot soup into them it warms them enough."

So did he, but he felt that she was scamping her attention to his supper tonight, especially when she said,

"I didn't have time to get any beer. We'll get some for the week-end."

She was turning over the potatoes with a fork when the telephone rang. It was in her small bedroom; she sprang to answer it.

"Will you just finish the potatoes."

He could, of course, hear every word she said. He knew at once by her eager, obliging tone that it was that damned police station. She came back.

"I've got to go on duty again at eight-thirty. We're short-handed, two people away sick, and they haven't traced the thieves' car. Never mind, we've got time for supper in peace. Oh, look out, you're burning the potatoes."

He snatched the pan off the ring and shook it.

"How long is this going on?"

"Is what going on? If you mean how long shall I be on duty, I don't know. You'll have to count me out for tonight."

"You don't sound as though you mind."

15

"Of course I mind, I've been looking forward to it all day, but I've got to do my job."

"No, you haven't, Mary. You could throw it up and marry me, and get some reasonable part-time job that wouldn't always be making extra demands on you."

"It wouldn't be so interesting."

"That's just it. You're hooked on it."

"I do like it. And what you call reasonable jobs are not easy to get."

"That's true, but you would get one. You're the sort of person that does."

"Yes, I think I probably could. But I don't want to come out of the police . . . especially now when I've just been promoted to the CID."

"Don't you want to marry me?"

"Now? Oh, darling, I just don't know."

"If you don't know you don't want to."

"No it isn't that. It's that I can't decide about anything so important in a few minutes."

Part of her mind was speculating with interest as to what they wanted her back at the station for, but she was touched by his distress. He looked like a cross little boy about to burst into tears.

"Look, Robbie, it's my week-end off. We shall have our Saturday night, and we can talk about it all then. I must change now and go up the Station. Leave the washing up."

He bloody-well would although ordinarily he would have done it for her. She threw her arms round him and hugged him. After a minute he returned her embrace. She stood in the doorway and watched him walk to the lift, calling out after him.

"Till Saturday."

3

THE BIG GATES of Hollycroft stood open; a sludge of dead leaves and churned-up gravel piled against the bottom of them suggested that they had been open for some time. The house was hidden from the road by the curve of the short drive. Rain drummed on the roof of the police car which Constable Williams was driving; dripping branches of untrimmed shrubs lashed the windows.

Mary tried to clear a path on the steamy glass.

"It doesn't look as though anybody is living here yet."

"It's evidently been sold, there's no sales notice up. Developers are so romantic, they often seem to buy properties that they will never have a hope of developing."

"Somebody has been trying to do some gardening."

The spacious garden sloped down from the side of the house towards a patch of wood where the trees were covered with ivy, and choked by elder and bramble bushes. In front of the house a rose garden had at some time been planted; it was now veiled in bindweed, but an attempt to clear it had evidently begun; a few rose bushes stood up starkly above the clutter; weeds lay in sodden, yellowing heaps on the path.

"The house isn't empty. I can hear a radio."

It was a tall, solid red-brick house, probably built about the end of the nineteenth century, and disfigured by lavish stone trimmings; the front door, unpainted for some time, was propped open by a wheelbarrow. A young man whose red jersey and tousled dark hair were whitened in patches by plaster came out with a bucket of rubble which he emptied half into the barrow, and half round it. He glanced incuriously at the police car with the uniformed policeman driving it, then went inside again. Corby got out.

"Williams, you might have a look round at the back. There

must be a garage, and some out-buildings in a place like this. It would be an excellent dumping ground, while there's nobody living here."

But as he and Mary walked up the front steps, he saw that he had been wrong. Beside the door was a panel of freshly painted wood showing six shining new bells, though a tangle of wires sticking out from just inside the door suggested that they were not yet all connected. The top four were however numbered and labelled. No 1 bore in its slot a card with "M. Ellis" neatly printed on it. In No 2 was a strip of bright blue notepaper, with "Mrs Rosa Spinelli" scrawled on it in an unsteady hand, No 3 had "Landon" printed on a bit of cardboard, and another name, "Grainger", pencilled in below it. The fourth bell boasted an elaborately printed card, with "Samuel Dutton, Director of Companies" in fancy printing, and the address of an office in the City.

"Some people seem to have been in the devil of a hurry to live here," Corby remarked.

He pushed the front door open on to chaos.

It was not easy to see what exactly was being done on the ground floor. The young man in the red jersey had picked up a cup of tea from one of the window-sills, and settled himself on the second step of the staircase to drink it. An older man in dirty white overalls was slapping mortar on to some bare bricks which seemed to be the beginning of an inner wall; a leggy boy, whose jeans and the top of his vest were covered with as many varieties of paint as an artist's palette, was inexpertly sawing a plank stretched across two trestles at the back of the hall. A radio halfway up the staircase was belting out a description of a tropical island with samples of its native music interspersed. Like any part of a house where builders had been at work the hall looked as though it would never be in order again. But it would be easy to hide gelignite or other explosives in.

"I'm sorry to disturb you," Corby said. "Would you mind turning your radio down for a few minutes."

18

The bricklayer, glancing at the radio as if surprised to find it on, switched it off.

"We're police making some routine inquiries in this district, there's my card. Can you tell me who is the owner of this house?"

"Sam Dutton. I thought it wouldn't be long before some of your lot were after him."

"We aren't after anybody in particular. Why do you think we should be after Mr Dutton?"

"He messes us up."

"Does he? How?"

"We never know when we're going to be paid. He's not here half the time."

"I see he's got an office in the City. Can't you get in touch with him there?"

"He's never there. There's a girl there sometimes who answers the phone, she never knows where he is or when he's coming. Sounds like a kid who doesn't know anything about anything. Dutton's got another house up in Yorkshire, but we don't know the address. We had a card saying he'd be coming down this week, but he may not come. If he's not here by Saturday we're leaving. We'd be better off on the dole than doing a big job like this and not getting paid regular for it."

"There are people living here already, aren't there? Are any of them in?"

"The old lady's in upstairs. Mrs Spinelli; she's lame, she don't go out much. The two on the first floor, Grainger and Landon, they both go to work. They've got a kid and there's a woman brings him home from school in the afternoon and looks after him till they come. I don't know if she's brought him back yet, has she, Harry?"

The boy, looking pleased to stop his sawing, nodded.

"I seen her taking the kid upstairs."

"There's someone called Ellis, isn't there?"

"He's unemployed. He does a bit of work in the garden here. Lucky if he gets paid for it."

"Is he in?"

"I think he's down the garden in the tool shed."

"You probably know from the TV that we're having a search round London to try and find out where the IRA bomb-makers are hiding or where they hide their explosives."

"Aye, I saw that. There's plenty of places to hide bombs round at the back in the yard here and in the old buildings. There's a pile of our rubbish there in the yard, but there's no explosives in it. It's all old wood and bricks and plaster and stuff."

"You don't know of anything unusual happening here."

"Without Dutton I don't reckon I do."

"Well thank you very much. I'm sorry to have interrupted your work."

The bricklayer nodded and with the air of one getting back to real life switched on the radio again.

4

"GO UP AND see if you can find out anything from the old lady, Mary. By the time you've done that some of the others may have come in. Williams and I will go round to the back, and search the out-buildings."

The staircase was thick with plaster dust, the bannisters were white with it. As Mary ran up she heard a child screaming on the landing above her. She recognized both fear and anger in the scream. As she reached the landing the noise stopped for an instant. A boy of about four or five years old came out of a room at the side. On seeing her he stood staring, tears running down his cheeks into his open mouth. A sharp-faced woman in a green mackintosh with a scarf tied over her head followed him.

"You naughty little boy, you! I'll smack you if you start that noise again."

She saw Mary and changed to an unpleasantly fawning tone.

"Now then, Guy, don't cry any more but just play quietly with all your nice toys till your mother comes. You won't be alone, the men are working downstairs.

"I want Mummy. I want Mummy."

"She'll be home in a minute. . . . Go back in there."

She gave the child a push so that he stumbled in through the doorway of the room, and evidently fell over something inside. He screamed again on a higher note of hysteria.

"You're not hurt, now." The woman eyed Mary curiously.

"Do you want to see Sylvia?"

"If she lives here I do. Is her name Grainger or Landon?"

"Grainger. Landon's the man she lives with. He's the boy's father. You don't know them, then?"

"No. I'm from the police. I have to make some routine inquiries about this house. Do you live here?"

"No thank you! I wouldn't be paid to live in this house with all the mess there is going on for ever. I just come in the afternoon to oblige. I fetch the boy from his little school, and stay with him till his mother comes home. She's late today and I've got an appointment with my dentist, so I'll be off now if you're going to wait here for Sylvia. Ta Ta Guy."

She made a perfunctory attempt to pat the boy's shoulder, but he jerked away from her. She hurried off down the stairs.

Mary knelt down to bring her face on a level with the child's.

"My name is Mary. May I stay with you till your mother comes home?"

He did not answer, but he stopped crying except for an occasional gulping sob. Mary smiled at him and wiped his face with her handkerchief. After studying her carefully for a minute he achieved a doubtful smile. He was a handsome upstanding boy, brown-eyed, brown-haired with a well-shaped head, and an open forehead.

"What shall we do till your mother comes? Will you show me some of your toys?"

This was not likely to be difficult as what must surely be most of them were lying on the floor of the big sitting-room, which was furnished with low chairs, a deep-seated sofa and small coffee tables. The one bookcase was mostly filled with paperbacks. There was a large music centre against the wall, and all the usual bottles stood on a low shelf that ran halfway round the room.

Mary sat down and picked up one of the toys.

"What a splendid truck. How does it work? Does it wind up?"

"Oh no. It's on batteries."

His face suddenly shone.

"There's Mummy."

The young woman who came quickly into the room was unmistakably Guy's mother, with the same brown eyes and rich curling hair, the same rounded forehead.

"I'm late, I know, darling. Where's Nancy?" She saw Mary.

"Did you come instead of her?"

"No, I just happened to come before she went."

"So she was going to leave you again, was she, Guy? We really shall have to find somebody else."

As the boy hugged her knees she looked over his head at Mary.

"Did you come to see me, or Rodney."

"Both of you, please, if possible. I'm from the police. I'm Detective Constable Copthorne. Here's my card. We're just making a few routine inquiries."

"Police! Are you a woman policeman? But you're not in uniform."

"No because I'm in the CID. Detectives. We don't wear uniform."

"I suppose if you did everyone would see you coming. But what do you want to ask me about? I haven't done anything,

22

at least nothing that would get me into trouble with you. I shouldn't think Rodney has unless it's something to do with parking his car? He does sometimes lose patience and put it where he feels inclined."

"No, it's nothing to do with the car. I expect you know that we're making a house-to-house search round London for places where the IRA could be making their bombs or hiding the material for them? We asked the public to let us know if they saw anything unusual going on anywhere and we had an anonymous letter saying that there was something odd happening in this house."

"Really? I don't think there is, not more than there would be in any house with people living in when it was half-finished. How surprising, an anonymous letter about this place! Well, I didn't write it anyhow. I hardly ever write letters. I haven't written to mother for a month. I must try and do it this weekend."

Guy tugged impatiently at his mother's sleeve.

"I'm hungry. I want my tea."

"All right, you shall have it now. Would you like a cup of tea, Constable? Is that the right thing to call you? Do sit down, it's all ready. I've only got to boil the kettle."

It seemed as likely a chance as any other of finding out something, if there was anything to find out.

"There are some more people living in the house already, aren't there?"

"Yes, Mrs Spinelli lives upstairs. She's the widow of an Italian, but she's English, she came back to this country after her husband died. She used to be a singer. I think she was quite famous. There's a young man called Mervyn Ellis in the other flat upstairs. He's been made redundant. I think he was in some kind of engineering. He gets a bit of work sometimes from the Job Centre, and he works in the garden here in a desultory sort of way. I don't think he's very good at it, but it's been neglected for so long it's in a mess, like the house.

"Sam Dutton, the developer who bought these two houses,

has the other flat on this landing. It's an odd sort of arrangement because we're all only temporary. When he's finished the house he'll have to sell it or sell the flats separately. We all got a fairly low rent because we all had to sign a document saying we would turn out when he was ready to sell. But he seems to be so short of money that he can't get anything finished, he hasn't even begun to convert Greenways, the other house down the road. But I don't think he'd have anything to do with IRA bombs. There's nobody here who would. Mrs Spinelli is very lame and doesn't go out much. She just goes across to the convent sometimes in the evening, for a service."

"Is she a Catholic?"

"I don't think so. She just likes going to see them I suppose. They do her laundry. I'm sure she wouldn't have anything to do with people making bombs. And Mervyn Ellis wouldn't; he's a bit wet but he's quite harmless. This milk seems to have turned, I hope you don't mind. I had to give what was left of yesterday's to Guy. I forgot to bring a fresh carton. Do you like being a detective?"

"Very much. I've only been one for three months."

"I should have thought it might be rather awful, you must have to interfere with people so much. I should hate that."

"We don't interfere with them unless they're doing anything against the law."

"But you must have to interfere with them to find out if they are, don't you?"

"Well, yes, sometimes. But it's nearly always to protect other people."

"Do you think there are bombs in this house?"

Mary saw the child's startled eyes.

"I shouldn't think so. We just have to make sure. I must go now and see Mrs Spinelli if she can talk to me."

"Do you want to see Rodney when he gets home?"

"I expect one of us would like a word with him."

24

"Well I'm glad you came. I've never met a woman policeman before. Goodbye. Be careful of obstacles on the stairs."

5

ON THE FLOOR above, the first door that confronted Mary was painted a deep blue-green, and had a brass door-knocker shaped like a dolphin. Above it on a painted scroll was the name Rosa Spinelli.

Cheered by seeing any attempt at decoration in this place Mary clapped the knocker, and waited so long that she concluded Mrs Spinelli must be out. She was turning away when she heard the bolt shot back, and the door slowly opened a few inches.

"Who is it?"

"I'm sorry to disturb you, Mrs Spinelli. I'm from the police, I'm Detective Constable Copthorne. I've just come to make a few routine inquiries." She thrust her hand through the narrow opening. "Here's my card."

The card was taken and there was a pause.

"I see; you'd better come in."

The door opened. Mary saw a very old woman in a long black velvet coat, rubbed and stained in several places. Its wearer had draped a purple scarf with silver fringes over her mass of grey hair, which still had dark streaks in it. The face beneath the scarf was carefully enamelled, but lines showed through, and the rouge was unevenly smeared on the cheeks. The vividly painted mouth drooped at one corner; one eye was half-covered by the fallen eyelid, but the other plentifully ringed with mascara, was still very bright.

"You're a detective, are you? You don't look old enough."

"I'm twenty-eight."

"I suppose that seems old enough for anything to you. But you don't look sharp enough to be a detective either. Well, I can't stand up here and talk to you. I must sit down. I can't imagine what you can want from me, but you'd better sit down too and tell me."

Mrs Spinelli trailed across the room dragging one foot. With obvious relief she lowered herself on to a long couch draped with a heavily embroidered silk shawl. She pointed to a chair near it.

"You don't have a uniform? I thought I'd seen pictures of them."

"I wore one when I was a WPC, a woman police constable. But detectives don't wear them."

"I should think you looked very nice in it. You're wise still to keep to plain lines, they suit you. What have you come to arrest me for?"

"I haven't come to arrest you for anything, Mrs Spinelli. Oh!" Mary broke off involuntarily. "I've never seen so many interesting things in one room."

It was a large room, but there was hardly a square foot of empty space on any of the walls. There were pictures, in some places so close together that they were almost touching one another. They were sketches of places, portraits, photographs of what looked to Mary like scenes from plays. Some of them were framed in dusty gold frames, others in light wood or aluminium. There were several mirrors in elaborate gilt or bronze frames. The shelves were filled with china, pottery, glass, and a big bookcase full of dusty books and musical scores nearly covered one wall.

"You can understand that this room is the despair of my home-help. You look rather dazed ·yourself. What is it you want to ask me?"

Mary repeated her story.

"I haven't made any bombs. I shouldn't know how to, I don't know anybody who does it. You can look round the rest of this flat if you like, but you won't find any explosives. And I certainly haven't written any anonymous letters. I have an old typewriter put away somewhere in this place, I don't know where, but I never use it now, and my handwriting could be recognized even if I tried to disguise it. So you can cross me off your list with an easy mind."

"You don't know of anybody in this house who might write an anonymous letter?"

"I hardly know anybody in this house at all except perhaps I might say I know the little four-year-old boy on the floor below, but he can't write yet."

"If you happen to see anything unusual going on in the house, would you be so kind as to ring me at the Blent Street Police Station? If I'm out would you ask for any other member of the CID."

"If there was anything unusual going on I should probably be the last person to see it. I don't go out of this flat much. When the conversion is finished and the flats are for sale I intend to buy this one, I could never contemplate moving all this stuff again. But yes, if I did come across anything suspicious I would ring you up. Please leave a note of the telephone number of your police station. Would you put it on my desk."

On the desk a large silver-framed photograph of a girl in a fantastic costume stood out above a clutter of lesser photographs, and letters opened and unopened.

The voice behind Mary said.

"Do you know who that is?"

"Isn't it you?"

"Perhaps you will make a detective after all."

"May I ask if you were an actress?"

"A singer. In opera mostly, though I did a good deal of concert work too."

"How thrilling! Is that a photograph of you in opera?"

"Yes, as the Princess in *Turandot*. An opera by Puccini. You probably haven't seen it."

"No, I'm afraid I haven't. I've only been to *Hansel and Gretel* and *The Marriage of Figaro*. We were taken in a party from school."

"Well, you made quite a good start. A pity not to go on, if you liked it."

"May I ask, are you an Italian?"

"Oh, no, I was born in Manchester. That's where I had my first singing lessons. I can't tell you about it now, you're busy. But if you like to come and see me again some time when you're not on duty . . . just for a cup of coffee—you can if you like."

"How marvellous! Of course I should like to. I've never met a great singer before."

"You are only meeting the remains of a good one now. Well, I suppose you must go and look for bombs somewhere else. Don't go too near them. Are you religious, by the way?"

"Not very, I used to go to church with my family, and I still do when I go home."

"You might find religion worth your attention, I myself have ignored it for too long, and now I have no certainty about anything. Be off with you. Au revoir."

6

CORBY AND PC Williams thankfully finished examining the heap of wet plaster, rotting wood, and broken bricks which the builders had piled up in the stable yard. Their van was the only vehicle in sight. In the part of the old stables which had been made over into a garage the sliding door was locked, but the door of what had probably been the harness room was open.

Corby straightened his back, and brushed off his waterproof as much of the sticky detritus as he could.

"Have a look inside, Williams, and see if you can get up into the loft. I suppose if Grainger and Landon have cars they are probably out at work in them and Dutton too, perhaps, unless he's in Bradford. We'll get the garage keys when somebody comes home. Meanwhile, just see if there's anything in the loft, and you might, while we're here, go round to the convent and ask leave to look at their out-buildings. Not that I suspect them of any bomb-making, but other people can hide things in the most innocent places. I'm going down the garden to look for this improbable character who may be spending an afternoon like this in the tool shed."

Corby squelched down the sodden path towards the wood. The tool shed, a solid brick building, was just on the edge of it. Swags of virginia creeper hung over its walls, there were still a few scarlet leaves clinging to the leafless stalks, which half-covered the small window, also obscured by cobwebs.

The entrance was evidently at the back. Corby walked round the shed and saw that the door had been taken off its hinges, and was lying just inside the wood in a gap between the trees where there had been an attempt at a clearance of bramble and ivy.

Taking the door off no doubt made the tool shed lighter, but must make it much colder. Corby was not surprised that the young man who swung round sharply at the sound of his footsteps, was wearing two old thick sweaters, the roll collar of one pulled up to his ears, and a woollen cap crushed down over his forehead.

He was sowing seeds in a wooden box full of earth, but he looked as startled and guilty as if he had been planting bombs. His blue eyes, good eyes in shape and colour, were red-rimmed, his lips looked dry and chapped, his nose was running. He wiped it with his sleeve and stepped back as if he expected Corby to hit him.

"Mr Mervyn Ellis?"

"Yes."

"I'm sorry I startled you. I'm police. Making a few routine inquiries. Chief Detective Inspector Corby. Here's my card."

The young man put out a hand coated with wet soil, and then hastily drew it back.

"I'd better not touch it. My hands are too dirty. But I don't understand. Is something the matter?

"Has there been an accident?"

"No, there's been no accident. I expect you know that we're searching all over London for places where the IRA might be making bombs or hiding the material for them."

An unmistakable relief spread over the young man's face.

"Oh, I see. Is that all?"

"All?"

"I mean it's nothing to do with me. I haven't ever seen a bomb, I don't know what they look like, nor exactly what they're made of."

"We had a letter suggesting that something unusual might be going on in this house."

"I suppose that whoever wrote that meant that the building was going on such a long time. The workmen do seem to have been here for ever. But that's because they sometimes don't get paid so they go away for a week or two."

"It must be very uncomfortable for you all. Why do you stay here?"

"Oh, because I like it. It's so convenient."

Corby looked out of the dirty window at the sodden garden.

"Is it?"

"Yes. There's so much room here and you can do what you like. Nobody interferes with you."

"Are you very fond of gardening?"

"No, not so very fond, but I do know a bit about it. And the flat is cheap till the rest of the house is finished. I'm using my redundancy pay for the rent now; it wasn't very big because I wasn't in the job long, but I hope when the flats are sold I might be able to keep mine and stay on as gardener and caretaker."

He picked up the trowel with a hand that trembled. He was blinking all the time. A very nervous young man, Corby thought, perhaps this place meant safety to him just because he had been here for a time and had made himself a feeling of home.

He was eager to talk now that Corby had somehow given him a kind of reassurance.

"I don't think anybody here would write an anonymous letter. They're all very nice people."

"Does that include the owner?"

"Sam Dutton? Oh, yes. He can't help it that he's run short of money, everything is so expensive nowadays, and the builders' wages are so high. But he'd never do any harm to anybody. And he's not Irish. He comes from Yorkshire. I think whoever wrote that letter must have made a mistake. It must really be some other house where there's something wrong."

"Well, will you let me know if you notice anything?"

"I will, I certainly will."

"I'll write down the telephone number of the Blent Street Station."

"You can write it on here."

Mervyn Ellis pushed a catalogue with an astoundingly bright picture of mixed daffodils on the back towards Corby, who scribbled the number on the margin.

"Who lives in the next house, Greenways? Has Mr Dutton bought that too?"

"Yes, but he hasn't started to convert it yet. He'll have to finish this one first, and then he'll have the money from selling the flats here to develop Greenways."

"So Greenways is empty now?"

"No, there are several people living in it. They're squatters or there were some squatters there. Now I think there are some people who publish a magazine."

"What kind of magazine?"

"I haven't seen it. I think it's political."

"You're not interested in politics?"

"Not in party politics. Only in the big issues, the nuclear threat."

"That like everything else is becoming an issue in party politics. Mr Ellis you're shivering with cold. You're surely not going to stay down here much longer? It will be dark soon."

"I know. But I've got one or two things to finish off. If you're going back to the house let me show you the side path up the garden, it's not nearly such a bog."

They walked up a narrow gravelled path past what had evidently been the kitchen garden. A beech hedge, broken down in one or two places, separated them from the convent garden next door. Through the gaps Corby saw the orderly beds, and neat paths.

"Somebody evidently looks after that place. I suppose they have a gardener. Does it make you envious?"

"Well, it does rather. But they don't have a gardener, the nuns do it themselves. There's an old one, Sister Veronica, who knows all about gardening, and she tells the younger ones what to do. Not that most of them are young . . . but they do work hard. Now you just go to the front door of Hollycroft by that path round the house."

"Many thanks."

"Perhaps I shall be seeing you again."

"I hope to finish here this afternoon, but perhaps you will."

7

IT WAS ALREADY dark as Corby and Mary Copthorne walked up the drive to Greenways. There was one lit window in the upper part of the house. By the light of Corby's torch they skirted a circular flower bed and arrived at the front door.

He rang the bell but there was no answer.

"There must be somebody in unless they've left one light on to look as though there was."

"Or gone out and forgotten to switch it off."

Corby rang again. After a minute the glass fanlight above the front door was illuminated, but nothing else happened.

Corby seized the old-fashioned iron knocker and banged it.

The door opened an inch at a time on a chain. A young female voice, Cockney and nervous, asked:

"Who's there?"

"Police . . . Just making a few routine inquiries in this part. Here's my card."

Holding his card through the narrow opening Corby at first felt nothing, then a gentle pull and the card was taken from him.

"May we come in and have a few words with you?"

"Yes, I think . . . I suppose it's all right."

The chain dropped . . . light fanned out as the door opened. There was no one in sight. In the segment of light outside Corby saw Mary with her hands thrust into the pockets of her anorak, and its hood pulled over her hair. She grinned at him. She was always cheerful company!

"You'd better come inside," the young voice repeated.

They stepped into a very cold hall, panelled halfway up the walls with wood which had been painted black, but from which most of the paint was peeling. The once-white walls above it were grimy; cobwebs hung from the moulding and long cracks ran across the ceiling.

The girl, standing there and staring at them, murmured uneasily.

"I hope they won't mind."

"Whoever 'they' are will surely know that it is always quite right to open the door to the police."

She was young and small with a straight fringe of dark hair which had evidently not been cut lately, it hung half over her eyes. She peeped up nervously through it. She seemed to be dressed in an assortment of rugs, whose fringes touched the floor. It was not surprising that she should have wrapped herself in anything that she could find for the chill dankness of the hall seemed even more penetrating than the raw afternoon outside.

"Are you alone in the house?"

"I am when the others are out. When I'm alone I'm always

33

afraid of opening the door. You don't know who may be trying to get in."

"It's very sensible to keep the chain on when you're alone and to make people account for themselves before you let them in. My name as you see on my card is Chief Detective Inspector Corby, and this is Detective Constable Copthorne. Is there some place a bit warmer than this where we could talk to you for a few minutes?"

"I could put the gas fire on in the office: it soon warms it."

"Then for heaven's sake let's go there."

She cut off a tremulous smile as if she was not sure that it was allowed to smile at the police. She led the way across the hall, opened a door, and stood aside to let them go in to a long room papered in dark red and looking as though it must once have been a dining-room. It now seemed to be an office; there was a typewriter on a small table; a desk; a pile of printed magazines, and another of typing paper. The girl snatched up a tray with three unwashed mugs on it, and carried it outside. She came back in a minute, and switched on the gas fire.

"Let's sit down, shall we?" Corby moved chairs up to the fire, and glanced at Mary who took out her note-book.

"What is your name?"

"Truda. Gertrude it is really. Gertrude Halton."

"Do you live here?"

"Yes; well I do just now."

"Who are the other people living here."

"I suppose it's all right for me to tell you?"

"If you didn't tell me I might wonder why and suspect that perhaps they were up to no good."

"Oh, no, its nothing like that. It's just that I don't like to do anything without asking them."

"Come along, Miss Halton. Who are they?"

"Shelton Gaines. He edits the magazine. And Toby Forrester. He's the Assistant Editor, he writes poetry. That's

34

why he's interested in the magazine, so that his poetry can be printed in it. I think his mother often pays for the printing."

"I expect she does. I see it's called, *Explosion*."

"That's just a name."

"May I look at a copy?"

"I'm sure you could have one. There are always some left."

Corby looked round the room, which in spite of the gas fire now scorching their legs, felt chilly and looked forlorn.

"Are you by any chance squatters?"

"No. Not now. We were for a bit when we first moved in. It's so difficult to find anywhere to live, and nobody seems to take any interest in these houses. Then Mr Dutton bought them, and asked us to pay rent. It's a small rent because we shall have to move out when he begins to turn this house into flats. But he can't get the work done on Hollycroft. I think he hasn't always got enough money to pay the builders. So we can stay on here for the moment."

"Do you work on the magazine too?"

"Yes, in a way. I don't write things. I answer the telephone and take messages, and I post copies to people. But I'm the housekeeper really. I do the cooking and shopping and as much cleaning as I can; it's such a big house. There are still some rooms I haven't even been into." She added nervously, "I do hope I haven't told you anything I shouldn't. You won't turn us out, will you?"

"I couldn't even if I wanted to, and why should I want to? You have a legal right to stay here as Mr Dutton's tenants. Anyhow that's not what I came about. I came because we were told in an unsigned letter that there was something unusual going on in Hollycroft. Do you know the people who are living there at present?"

"No, I've never been inside Hollycroft. Mr Dutton came here once when he found we were living—well—squatting here, but I only just saw him when I opened the door to him. From my bedroom window upstairs I can see into the garden next door, and I've sometimes watched a young man working

35

there, and once or twice a little boy running about. But Shelton goes up there to pay the rent."

"May I ask, do these two young men pay you for your services?"

She flushed an uncomfortable red, and replied with more spirit than she had seemed capable of.

"I don't see why you have to ask me that."

Corby, who had his answer, replied, "No, well I won't."

She exclaimed, "I hear the car coming now. So you can ask them what you want. I'll go and get them."

One of her rugs fell off as she hurried to the door, which she shut behind her. Mary picked up the rug, folded it neatly and hung it over the back of a chair.

"She wants to warn them about us."

"Unless they're up to something she doesn't know, they haven't got anything to worry about. But squatters or people who have been squatters get a habit of feeling uneasy. They're exploiting her all right."

"Yes, but I think she likes it."

The warning or whatever the consultation in the hall lasted a minute or two. . . . Corby flicked over the pages of the magazine.

"What is it like?"

"Activist Left. According to pattern. There are several poems by T. Forrester. Mother, of course, as we heard, pays the printer. I'm not a judge of poetry. I wonder if she likes the title?"

The door opened and two young men came in escorted by Truda, who looked much more confident now that her allies were here.

"This is Shelton, and this is Toby."

Shelton, who came first had a long, narrow, pale face, light hair brushed smoothly back and looked, Mary thought, as though he fancied himself, and expected everyone else to fancy him. The poet was a plump young man with a tousled head of brown hair, eyes and mouth ready to smile. He wore a red jersey, and dirty jeans. Shelton was in a neat if rather shabby suit. He pulled up a chair and sat down.

"Good evening, Chief Inspector. What can we do for you? Truda tells me you are interested in our magazine. Perhaps you would like to subscribe to it? But you must let us give you a free copy first so that you can see if you like it."

"Thank you but I haven't come here about the magazine. In fact I didn't know it existed."

"That's a very unkind thing to say. But perhaps you are not interested in politics. You are one of the people who get more money from the present Government instead of less."

Corby ignored this and explained his errand.

"Oh, I see, well, we've got no bombs here. None of us would want to write an anonymous letter. I have far too many letters from our readers to answer, without burdening myself with unnecessary correspondence; Toby doesn't write prose; it bores him. I suppose this letter is written in prose?"

"Of course."

"There's no 'of course' about it. We have had two letters in verse addressed to the magazine. And as for Truda, she's far too busy doing really useful things in this house to want to waste her time writing silly letters."

Truda smiled widely at this accolade.

"Do you see much of the people in Hollycroft?"

"Hardly anything. Sam Dutton is our landlord, and I have a drink with him when I go and pay the rent. We shall have to leave here when he starts converting this house. If he ever does, he's been long enough on the other one. He's away a good deal, he's got a house in Yorkshire."

Corby rose to go.

"It's too dark now for us to do the routine check on the out-buildings of this house, but we shall come to it on our search of this district."

"Come when you like. There's an old stable at the back where we keep Toby's car. There's a lot of rubbish about in the yard but you won't find any bombs there, which makes me feel free to admit that there are a good many people in this country that I shouldn't mind using a bomb on. You have to disapprove of that of course."

"If you'd ever been where a bomb exploded among a lot of people, Mr Gaines, I think you might disapprove of it too."

"I can't tell that, can I, till it happens. Has Truda offered you a drink? But you mustn't have one, of course. Do keep that copy of the magazine. Please don't leave it behind, people do sometimes and it's so hurtful to our feelings."

As the front door slammed rather than shut behind them, Corby exclaimed: "Damned irritating young Jackanapes!"

"Yes. I wanted to smack him."

Corby laughed and felt better.

"We'll go back to Hollycroft now and if Dutton and Landon haven't come in we'll get Williams to drive us to the Station. You'll have to come up here again when you're doing the round. But I don't believe Shelton's a bomb-maker. He doesn't attempt to cover his tracks. And there's nothing Irish about any of them. The one thing that all the inhabitants of these two houses have in common seems to be that they're in transit. They don't expect to be here long."

"Mrs Spinelli does. She says she could never move again."

"Then I hope she has a good solicitor to look at whatever document Dutton asks her to sign. Oh God, here's the rain again."

"I'm sorry it has been such a disappointing day for you when you so seldom get out of the office."

"Disappointing days are two-thirds of police work. You don't know that yet."

"No, because I enjoy all of it."

"You're a good girl, Mary. It's a long time since you've been to see us at home."

"I was waiting till Jessica came back for the vacation."

"Don't wait. Come and talk sense to Tilly."

38

"I don't think she'd like that. I can't be a police-woman off-duty."

"No, your boy-friend wouldn't like it."

"He doesn't much like my being one on duty."

"They don't always. We've lost one or two promising WPC's that way. But we mustn't lose you that way, Mary. Your young man will have to get used to it."

Mary laughed. "Oh, yes he will. I don't want to let anything stop me being a police-woman."

8

THE BUILDER'S VAN stood outside the front door of Hollycroft, but the men were still inside drinking a last cup of tea in the hall. PC Williams was sitting on an upturned crate, his helmet on his knee and a mug in his hand. An experienced and friendly copper, he would have learned anything the builders could tell him. Corby was just going to call him to drive them back to the station, when the lights of another car swept round the bend of the drive. It was coming much too fast and pulled up with a squeal of brakes a yard from the builder's van.

The car door opened and a suitcase fell out. It was followed by the bulky figure of a man wearing what in the light from the doorway was obviously a beautiful and expensive camel-hair coat. Above its collar was a creased red neck, and a bald head with a fringe of ruffled, grey hair.

"I suppose you thought I wasn't coming."

The new arrival extracted a brief case and a stuffed canvas bag from his car. He aimed a kick at the suitcase.

"Well, pick it up one of you. You don't think there's a bomb in it, do you?"

Williams picked up the suitcase and carried it indoors.

"Hallo! Police here! What's happened?"

Corby stepped forward and proferred his card.

"Mr Dutton? Nothing has been happening here, Sir. We've been making some general inquiries, that's all. Here's my card. Can I have a word with you?"

"Of course, of course. Do you mind if I just pay these men first? They've been waiting three weeks for it."

He opened his despatch case and handed out sealed packets.

"There you are. Be off with you now, but be sure to turn up in good time on Monday morning. Don't lie in for half a day to recover from the weekend as you generally do. I may be going North again, and I want to go over the work with you first."

He turned to Corby.

"Now then, Inspector, at your service. Come up to my flat."

"There's still a right mess here," he said as he led the way upstairs. "It ought to have been finished by last Christmas, but of course it wasn't anywhere near. As you can see if it's finished by next Christmas I shall be lucky. You can't get anything done quickly nowadays, that's what the banks don't seem to realize, nor the government either. We hear a lot about them all wanting to help enterprise and small businesses but bloody hell do they."

On the first-floor landing he took out his keys and opened the door on the left.

"This is my own flat at present but I shall probably let it later on when the place is finished. I might sell the whole house if I get a good offer. Come in."

He switched on a galaxy of lights, including a modern— and in Corby's opinion—a very ugly chandelier in the middle of the room. The effect was dazzling. The walls were covered with an embossed and gilded paper. Two big chairs and a sofa were upholstered in brocade of the same design and colour. The only other furniture was a magnificent grand piano with a big bowl of dead flowers standing on it; a cocktail cabinet, and an ordinary flat-topped office table pushed away in one corner.

40

"I know I can't offer you a drink, Chief Inspector, but you won't mind my having one? Do sit down."

Dutton filled a tumbler with whisky, and sank into one of the shining chairs.

"I wish I was in the police! I've put on half a stone in the last six months. It's worry, that's what it is. I know it makes some people thin but it just makes me drink more."

"These are worrying times."

"Nothing has gone right with these houses. To begin with I wanted to buy the three, but the one up the road is a convent, and the nuns have got a long lease. Not that I wanted to turn them out, or not before I had to. I've a great respect for them. There's plenty of room in the world today for good women, and good men too when you think how many bad ones there are. Do you play the piano, Inspector?"

"No, I don't. One of my daughters plays quite well."

"I wish I'd learnt to when I was a lad. Not that you need it now with TV and radio and all that, but you must have a piano in a room like this. It wouldn't look anything without one."

"Mr Dutton, I'm sure you know that we are making a house-to-house search around London for any premises where the IRA might be making bombs or storing the materials for making them?"

"I do know, and I'm sorry for you. Why you could hide a stick of gelignite in a child's sock."

"They need other explosives and detonators too, of course. But you're quite right; it's a near-impossible job."

"You need a few reliable tip-offs to get anywhere at all."

"We've just had one about this house."

"This house! But that's a load of rubbish! Who from?"

"It's anonymous."

"What the bloody hell did it say?"

"That as the police had asked members of the public to report any unusual behaviour that they noticed, the writer of

41

this letter felt it right to mention some might be noticed in Hollycroft Grange."

"That's absurd! There's nobody in this house who would get mixed up with the IRA. The letter's been written by a nutter. They always are. I've had anonymous letters in my time, but I've never taken any notice of them."

"We have to take notice of everything."

"Of course you do, of course. Don't think I'm criticizing you. I'm on your side. 'God help the police' is the way I look at it. All sorts of people get rough with them, and they're expected to handle them with kid gloves. By the way, you must come across a lot of different people in your job. You don't know of anybody who would like to put his name down for a luxury flat in this house? Fine large rooms, beautiful garden free for all to sit in, or to garden in if they like, I've got an idea we might run that on communal lines. And we're goint to make a swimming-pool at the far end of the garden where that bit of wood is. It's an advantage that wood, it cuts this place right off from the housing estate in the summer. You might think you were in the depths of the country, and it's only four and a half miles from Piccadilly Circus."

"I don't know anyone at the moment looking for a flat of this kind. You say that none of the people in this house would be likely to have anything to do with the IRA. What about your tenants in Greenways?"

"Perfectly harmless. Perfectly harmless. Oh I know that magazine of theirs is called *Explosion*, but that's only to try and draw attention to it, and you've got to do a lot more than that nowadays to draw attention. Nobody reads the thing anyhow. I don't think they've published a number lately, probably can't afford to pay the printers. If they had anything to do with bombs they wouldn't be such fools as to call the rag *Explosion*, now would they?"

"I shouldn't think so but I want to know a bit more about them."

"They were squatting in Greenways when I bought these

two houses. You know how it is, it's not easy for the young nowadays to find places where they can afford to live. They're well-educated too, these lads. They'd only been squatting in Greenways for a few months when I bought it. Shelton Gaines had been living in a big squat in some derelict house that belonged to the council, and was due for demolition, so they sent the police in early one morning, and evacuated the lot. Well you know how it is, it still goes on all over, though of course it isn't news now, people have got tired of hearing about it.

"Anyhow Gaines, Shelton Gaines, who is a shrewd fellow, had got wind of the police coming, and he'd been looking round at empty houses, and come across these. The other lad Toby Forrester met Shelton when he went to the council-house squat to try and write an article about it. Or it may have been a poem. I don't know exactly what he writes. I don't think he makes much money by it. He was in some wretched lodging and was glad enough to move into Greenways with Gaines.

"They're not squatting now. I make them pay a small rent, and I've made them sign a paper to say that they'll get out as soon as the conversion work starts on the house. And when that will be God only knows! But after all it's better for a house to be occupied than to stay empty. They keep a bit of heat going, and now they've got this girl with them, she does some cleaning. I shouldn't have had so much trouble with Hollycroft if it hadn't been unoccupied for several years. We've got to help one another out when we can. Are you married, Chief Inspector?"

"Yes."

"Happily?"

"I think so. I hope my wife does."

"There's not many of them satisfied. They're too good, or they think they are and their husbands can't match it. And they don't want their husbands to launch out and have a bit of enterprise. Not the one I married anyway. I'd have done

43

better if she believed in me and backed me, but you can't alter folk, they're the way they're made."

"If you do happen to notice any unusual behaviour either here or in Greenways will you give me a ring at Blent Street Station?"

"I certainly will. I'll be glad to help. I'm only here part of the time. I've got another house in Bradford—fine house in a residential part of the town, three reception rooms, five bedrooms, two bathrooms, garage, garden, all in nice order. When I say it's my house it belongs strictly speaking to my wife. Her father owned it and left it to her. I should like to sell it to help to pay for this work here, but she won't, she has a sentimental feeling for it. It's natural, isn't it?"

Corby thought it might be sensible as well as natural.

"Well, thank you, Mr Dutton. Here's the telephone number of the police station. I'm sorry to have disturbed you as soon as you got home."

"Not at all. It's a pleasure to meet you. If you're going now I'll come down with you and show you where the light switches are on the stairs. They've put them in the wrong places of course. They did them when I wasn't there."

The landing light revealed a woman walking slowly ahead of them down the staircase, a tall figure in a long black coat with a scarf over her hair. She was obviously having difficulty in lowering one foot each time to the next step. One hand clutched the bannister, the other held a tall, old-fashioned umbrella which did not look strong enough to provide support. The light was poor and there was something ghostly in the slow-moving figure.

"Mrs Spinelli. Mrs Spinelli," Dutton called out. "Don't go any further till I put the next light on. Are you going out on a night like this? Have you got a car ordered?"

"No, I am only going round to the convent. I have a torch, and if it is still raining the Mother Superior will allow one of the sisters to walk back with me with an umbrella."

"Wait a minute. I'll run you round there now in my car.

It's at the door. You've met the Chief Inspector? I hope you were able to satisfy him that you were not making any bombs?"

"Good evening, Inspector. Your . . . is she your assistant? the girl detective came to see me, a nice girl but I should have thought not sharp enough to be a detective."

"She's good at her job, Mrs Spinelli."

Dutton opened the front door, helped her into his car and turned round.

"Good night, Inspector. I'm afraid you've spent an afternoon here for nothing, but I hope you'll have better luck the next place you go to."

His car lights swept the dripping branches of the dark drive, and vanished.

"Back to the station now, Williams. Where's Copthorne?"

"The other tenant in the first floor flat came home, Sir. She went up to see him."

9

IT WAS COLD in the hall and quiet after the builders had gone. Mary sat on a low step of the staircase, leaning against the bannisters; if it had been just a little warmer, she would have dropped off to sleep. PC Williams sat patiently on the crate. Mary roused herself.

"Did you go round to the convent?"

"Yes. The Head Nun sent word that I was to see anything I liked. There wasn't anything to see. There's a laundry-room with two washing machines, and a warm cupboard full of clean laundry they'd done. Then in the old stables next to it there's a small car that some of them run the Head Nun about in and the laundry van, all as clean as a whistle. There's nothing else but some garden tools, and a lot of plaster figures that they use for the crib at Christmas . . . life-sized figures, Mary and the Baby and Joseph, and a lot of angels with wings painted gold. They were all covered with plastic sheets, but the nun pulled them back for me to look where I wanted. But nothing there of course."

The front door opened and a young man in a smartly cut mackintosh came in, carrying an umbrella and a brief-case. He slammed the door, glanced at Mary and with more curiosity at Williams in his uniform.

"Hallo. Anything wrong here?"

"No Sir. A routine check."

He ran upstairs, and they heard another door bang.

"That'll be Landon."

"Yes, I should think so. I'd better go up and see him. I'll give him a minute or two to settle down."

He had kicked up a cloud of dust from the stairs. Mary brushed it off her shoulders and wiped her face, wondering how long the tenants of the flats were going to have to put up with this. She was not surprised that tempers should be ruffled when she heard a door opened above her and the sound of quarrelling voices.

"Why couldn't you get it on your way home? You'd only just have had to go a little way up Cheriton Street."

"I thought it would be less trouble to wait till I could have the car. There wasn't much of yesterday's milk left and Guy upset it all at tea-time."

"Then he should go without."

"You can't punish children like that, they need fresh milk."

"One of the many ways in which they make damned nuisances of themselves."

Guy felt it due to himself to give a piercing scream.

"Oh get along, but be quick. I want dinner early, I may be going out again after it."

"Where to?"

"Anywhere where I can get a little peace."

"The builders have gone now."

"I don't mind the builders."

Sylvia came running downstairs, jumping Guy from step to step.

"If you want to see Rodney", she said to Mary, "he's at home now. I don't know that you'll find him in a very co-operative mood."

Mary went up, Sylvia had left the door half-open. Mary knocked but there was no answer. She tried again and an unwelcoming voice called out: "Come in".

Rodney had poured a drink, and settled himself in an armchair with his legs over the arm. He took them down, frowning at the intruder. He was, Mary thought, very nice-looking, dark, lean, long-limbed.

"Hallo. Do you want Sylvia? She's just gone out."

"No thank you. I saw her earlier in the afternoon. I shall be very glad if you can spare me a few minutes."

She handed over her card and explained her errand. Rodney looked carelessly at the card and handed it back to her.

"I don't know what you want me for. Sylvia will have told you anything about our affairs that you need to know. More, probably, she has no idea of reticence. Will you have a drink? I suppose not. Who's to know if you do? Anyhow that would be all I could do for you. I don't know anything about bombs. I've never met any of the IRA. I can't imagine that anybody in this house would be likely to write an anonymous letter. Better try Greenways, that's the next house down the road. There are one or two shady characters in there. At least I should think they are shady. I really don't know much about it."

His tone was clearly dismissive. Mary proferred the usual request, would he ring them up if he noticed anything unusual.

"I don't see why I should do your work for you."

"Wouldn't you be glad to help us to find out where bombs may be coming from? Anybody could be in danger from them. You could. Your little boy could."

47

"Yes, he could, couldn't he?"

She felt disconcerted as if she might have made a mistake. Perhaps Guy was not his child at all. She wrote on her notepad and tore off the page.

"Here's the telephone number of the Blent Street police station. Perhaps you would keep it in case you do want us. Please ask for anybody in the CID. Goodbye."

Well, not much prospect of help there. How surprising that Sylvia seemed to be happy! Rodney was not a person she herself would ever want to live with. She did not suspect him of making bombs or hiding explosives, but she was glad to get out of the room.

PART TWO

10

THE EARLY DARK of the November day had fallen by the time that Mervyn Ellis returned to the tool-shed. He knew that it was really no good going back there, but an obsession drove him on; he knew that he would not feel at ease, probably would not be able to sleep if he went indoors without doing at least a little work on his own project.

He went into the tool-shed by the small light of his pocket torch, but he had a lantern there with a thick candle in it. He lit it and hung it on a nail outside the doorway. He went to the cleared space just inside the wood where the door of the tool-shed was lying. He always found it an effort to move it, but he managed to drag it a yard or two. Where it had lain the dim light showed a large hole in the ground. Mervyn shone his torch into it, and climbed down the four steps that he had cut and strengthened with broken pieces of brick and wood from the builders' refuse in the yard. He was making another step, and started with much difficulty to scrape out the sticky clay.

Heavy rain began to fall again. Soon he could feel it through his two thick jerseys; it was no use trying, he would have to give up. Although he had only done a little he felt better for doing it. But oh, what a long job it was, and how was he going to be able to raise the money he would need for the whole thing? He replaced the door, put the tools back in the shed and squelched up the garden path towards the house.

He slipped and fell on the path, scraping his knee. As he got on to his feet again he was shaken by a passion of rage. These passions were recurring, they swept up like thunder out of a clear sky, and frightened him because they almost sent him reeling; they made his heart beat so fast that he could hardly breathe, and his head felt so tight that he was afraid it would burst. He was unhappy, sure that this must be very bad for him. The late-born child of middle-aged parents, who had neither humour nor enterprise, he had taken over from them the habit of worrying endlessly over his own health and behaviour. They had not by then expected to have children, and though they thought they were pleased they took a gloomy view of him. He did not remember the occasional rages of childhood which had devastated the stagnant home. They only came to the surface now when he was alone.

"That policeman, detective or whatever he calls himself! Coming here and accusing me of making bombs, and writing anonymous letters! If he was any good at all at his detecting job he would see that I'm not that sort of person! They've got to find somebody to blame or they won't get promotion; that's what it is.

"I'll write to my MP. I won't put up with any more persecution. I'll write to the Council for Civil Liberties. The police can't do whatever they like nowadays. We all know they're Fascists; I'll write a letter about him to BBC Television, they always keep an eye on what everyone is doing. I'll get that bloody Inspector demoted, or reprimanded anyhow."

But as he squelched up the garden his anger went down in him like boiling milk taken off the ring. When he reached the front door he saw that the police car was still there. It was Dutton's fault. Why didn't he look after the place properly, then there wouldn't be these absurd suspicions about it? You couldn't blame the police really, they had to do their job. He opened the front door with his key and trudged upstairs. One comfort, he couldn't with his muddy boots make them dirtier than they were already.

As he reached the first landing he saw Rodney Landon

standing in the doorway of his flat and frowning. Mervyn immediately felt that something he had done must have caused the frown. He was relieved when Rodney stopped scowling, and called out in a friendly way.

"Hallo, Ellis! You haven't been gardening on a day like this? You must be frozen. Come in and have a drink on your way up."

Mervyn was delighted by this unexpected invitation. He did not know that Sylvia and Rodney had just had a sharp exchange, and that she had flounced into the kitchen and banged the door, so that Rodney was glad of a diversion. The room was warm and brightly lit. Sitting in a comfortable chair with a glass of whisky, which he hardly ever drank, in his hand, Mervyn thought what a very nice fellow Rodney was, and agreed with every word he said almost before they were spoken.

"Must be an awful job gardening in this place," Rodney said. "I hope our landlord pays you plenty for it."

"Well, not yet. Mr Dutton is going to pay me something, but he hasn't yet."

"Don't you let the old rascal get away with that. Just down tools until he does pay."

Mervyn, who was not in the least likely to do anything of the sort, hastened to agree with Rodney.

"I expect I should. Yes, I think I really must."

"Did a police girl come to see you today?"

"I didn't see a girl. The policeman who was here, Chief Detective Inspector Corby, came down to see me in the toolshed."

"You were highly honoured, or specially suspected. I don't suppose you had written an anonymous letter, had you? To say that there was some sort of mayhem going on in this house?"

"No, of course I hadn't. I told him that none of the people in this house would do anything against the law."

"That's a rash statement to venture nowadays. They

53

thought we were making bombs for the IRA you know, or storing the material."

"Did they really? But there wouldn't be anything like that going on here. Of course not."

Guy, who was sitting on the floor fitting some pieces of Leggo into a shape, suddenly remarked, "But it's the Russians who are making bombs to throw at us."

Rodney looked down at the brown head and the busy hands.

"What do you know about it?"

"It's on television."

"Your mother lets you see too much TV."

"No she doesn't. Nancy likes to watch it. Besides of course I can turn it on for myself now when I want to."

Rodney shrugged. "I suppose children don't lead sheltered lives nowadays. What's the matter, Ellis?"

"I-I hope you'll excuse me. I must go now. I-I've got a letter to write."

"An anonymous one?"

"No, no, of course not. Its just that I—I feel rather seedy. I think I did too much gardening in the rain."

"Have another drink, that will put you right."

"No, thank you very much for this one. It's just that I must go up to my flat now if you don't mind."

"Of course not."

Sylvia came out of the kitchen followed by enticing smells of cooking food. She was smiling, she had forgotten all about the quarrel.

"I thought there was somebody here. I heard voices."

"Ellis was having a drink but he suddenly bolted. Perhaps he was going to be sick, he looked like it."

"It's just as well, because supper's nearly ready, and we couldn't have asked him to stay for it, there wouldn't be enough."

"Anyhow we don't want him."

54

11

DUTTON'S LIFT MEANT that Rosa Spinelli arrived at the convent ten minutes before her usual time, which anyhow was always a little early for Vespers. She longed for the chance of a brief conversation with the Mother Superior, whom she sometimes met in the corridor on her way to the chapel. It did not matter that they generally only exchanged a few words on an indifferent subject; even a sentence about the weather was comfort and reassurance. Reassurance was in the folds of the Mother's gown, and in her quiet voice, which although she had now lived for twenty-five years in England still kept her French inflection. Between her and Rosa there was an unexpressed consciousness of having been at home in other countries. Occasionally . . . very occasionally, Rosa asked to see the Reverend Mother if she had a problem about which she thought it could be considered worth while to consult her. Rosa had in her day been much loved and admired, her company sought after, but she rated her claim to the Mother's attention low because she was not a Catholic, because she was old and slowed down by the stroke which had made her ugly; so at least it seemed to her, especially as she remembered the days of her beauty, though nobody else now did.

She made her halting way along the corridor towards the chapel, hearing in the quiet only the tap of her own stick on the stones. The doors along the passage were all shut, but suddenly one flew open, to emit the shrill sound of quarrelling voices. Quarrelling was such an unusual sound in this place that Rosa stopped, disconcerted.

One of the nuns was Sister Maria, an old woman known to Rosa by sight; she sometimes scuttled in to the chapel to fill up the altar vases with water just before the sisters came in to Vespers. The other was a young nun with bright dark eyes, and a face flushed with anger, to the edge of her coif. Rosa had not seen her before.

"You cause the greatest inconvenience," the young nun was saying. "I have always to be careful that I deliver the laundry at exactly the time I have promised. If I do not come then the customers want to go out, they will not wait, they do not get their clean things till the week after, and so they are annoyed and look for another laundry . . . and all this because you cannot have the clean things ready for me when it is time to start the round."

The old nun sounded as though she was almost crying.

"Sister I am sorry, I do my best. This week there were so many blankets, large and heavy, I could not fold them quickly nor get them all into the boxes."

"No, because you start too late. . . ."

There was a step behind Rosa, and a sudden silence in the doorway. The Mother Superior's crisp tones cut into the quiet.

"What is this noise? Have you forgotten that it is forbidden to talk in the passages, and especially so near the chapel?"

The two nuns bent their heads, ashamed. The younger one spoke first.

"I am sorry, Reverend Mother. It was I who began it, but each week now the same thing happens, when I come to collect the clean clothes and put them in the van they are not ready in the boxes. I am late for our customers who are expecting me at a certain time, and so the laundry gets a bad name."

"Is this true, Sister Maria?"

The older nun could not speak for a minute, but she managed to choke down her tears. "There were so many blankets this time, Reverend Mother, and it is difficult to fold them quickly, they are too big for the boxes."

"Perhaps you need some help. I will speak to Sister Veronica about it and we shall see. It is necessary, of course, to discharge any business with the outside world punctually and accurately or they will think that the religious are not practical. . . . You, Sister Catherine, are quite right to be particular about this, but not to make a scene in the corridor, and to speak unkindly to a sister who has been here much longer than you have. You will apologize to Sister Maria."

The young nun, redder than ever in the face, murmured something of which the only audible word was "Pardon".

"Now you had better both go to your duties, it is not yet quite time for the service." She smiled a little and laid a hand on the young nun's arm.

"*Pas trop de zêle, mon enfant, pas trop de zêle.* We shall see about the blankets."

She waved them both away. They vanished willingly through the side door. Rosa had kept back, feeling that she ought to have got away from the little scene more quickly than she could. But *Mère* Jeanne had seen her.

"Ah, Madame Spinelli, you have come to join us even on such a *villain* evening. I hope you didn't get wet on the way here?"

"I was lucky, *ma mère*, I got a lift in a car from our door to yours."

"That is good; if it is still raining like this after Vespers Sister Clotilde shall walk back with you and take the big umbrella with which she goes to feed the hens."

"I hope it will be fine by then. I do not want to cause any inconvenience to anyone."

"Not at all, Madame, we are always pleased to see you. Now I must leave you, I have just time to write a letter before Vespers. Good night."

In the chapel Rosa, who could not kneel any more than she could pray, settled herself in her usual place, the chair at the end of the back row. A nun came in to light the candles on the altar; she went to the organ, switched on the light above it and began to play a voluntary. Rosa let her eyelids fall over her eyes. She did not go to sleep, but her mind wandered dreamily back into her past, shifting from one memory to another.

Some of the early ones were so sharp and clear, other more recent ones had faded. The kitchen of the house in Manchester where she patted a piece of dough with fingers that, however carefully she washed them, always made it dirty was much more vivid than many of the theatres all over Europe and America in which she had sung. She had been a good singer if not the prima donna that she and some of her teachers had expected of her. Sometimes now when she wanted to recall her happy hours in theatres and concert halls there seemed to be a high wall between her and them, as high as the wall at the bottom of the Villa Le Tavernule where you could lean over to look at the distant towers of Florence, or to pick capers from the plants that grew between the stones. What she would have liked to recall most often and most clearly, the years of her great happiness with Richard in the Villa, sometimes seemed to be veiled, whereas there was no veil over the struggling years of her second marriage with Claudio Spinelli.

Richard and Claudio were both dead, and now she was alone, her daughter, her only child and Richard's, far off in California. But Gelsomina was much less in her thoughts than the little boy, Guy, downstairs at Hollycroft. He and the Mother Superior were the two illuminated figures in her life.

But I shall never see Guy grown up, and there will be so many evenings when they will sing Vespers in this chapel and I shall not be here. The terror that was like a cold mist hanging round all her days crept nearer to her; she felt its chill invading her peace. They were only palliatives, her slender contact with the Mother, Guy's occasional visits to her flat, the sight and sound of him in the house.

She could not believe and there was no help for her. There was only the terrifying prospect of complete extinction, or the equally terrifying prospect of finding herself in some unknown form in an entirely unknown existence. These terrors did not often assail her so strongly in the chapel. Movement, or the most casual talk with another human being generally pushed

58

them a little further away from her. For once she was glad when the nuns walked out two by two down the aisle, and out of the chapel, and it was a positive comfort as she slowly followed them to see Sister Clotilde with the big carriage umbrella under her arm, and a broad smile on her simple face.

As soon as they were out of the building, and the umbrella was hoisted Sister Clotilde exclaimed excitedly. "Oh, Madame Spinelli did you know that we had a visit from the police this afternoon? Just fancy! They were looking for bombs!"

12

CORBY WAS SO well used to coming into the Station that he knew as soon as he pushed open the main door whether things were quiet, or whether there was any particular crisis. At the end of this afternoon all the telephone bells seemed to be ringing at once, and the place echoed with hurried footsteps and banged doors. Corby stopped at the desk.

"What's up, Sarge?"

The Station Sergeant replaced the receiver. "Missing child, sir."

"Oh, God!"

It was the incident that they all most dreaded, and that so far their district had escaped, though they had been called in to help with a neighbouring search, and it was one of their dog handlers who had found the raped and strangled body under the leaves piled up for burning in the public park.

"Mr Etheridge wanted to see you as soon as you came in, Sir."

Etheridge was a recent appointment to a job which Corby had half-wanted for himself, only half because he had always preferred detective work to anything else, but he was forty-seven and expected to be the head of a station before he retired. Lately he had felt that he was putting less energy into his CID work; not that he had neglected anything or failed to bring off anything that he could reasonably expect to come off, but he had done it by technique and application. The drive from inside, which really determined whether detective work, and probably any other work, was brilliant or good, was somehow not there any more. Etheridge, two years younger, had a drive from inside all right, but it was a different one, it was the push to get on which you must have, of course you must, but in Corby's opinion if that came first you were second-rate. He knew himself on his own level to be something like an inspired detective; during the last few months he had felt himself to be only a capable and experienced one. He had often noticed that even that youngster, Mary Copthorne, had the spark that he, perhaps only for the time being, had lost. All this flicked through his mind as he went up the stairs to Etheridge's room; it often came up at odd moments; it was so near the surface.

When he went into the room and saw Etheridge sitting behind his table with the light from the angle-poise lamp full on his papers, irritation stirred in Corby. The man was too smooth, too polished-looking, had to much of an almost military smartness, but he spoke cordially.

"Ah, there you are, Frank, I'm glad you're back. There's a girl missing. Clara Westerby. Thirteen years old. Lives in Cumberland Drive, and goes to the Answold Comprehensive. She set off at the usual time this morning to walk the three-quarters of a mile to school, and hasn't been seen since. She generally meets a friend on the way. Friend was late, and supposed Clara hadn't waited for her. No one discovered that she wasn't at school until the second lesson after lunch, which was a rehearsal of a play she had a part in. They telephoned her home to know if she was coming. Her mother, of course, was frantic at once; she said there was nothing wrong with Clara that morning except a few routine grumbles. She was pleased to have a part in the play, and was looking forward to the rehearsal. We've seen the headmaster and her form-mistress, and the girl who sits next to Clara in class; none of them had noticed anything unusual about her during the last week.''

"We've rung all the hospitals and now we're doing a house-to-house enquiry along her route; especially in the sweet-shops. There are two or three where the children often spend their dinner money in the morning—and then say at school that they weren't given any money, I suppose.''

"I'll go round to her home and see if the parents have remembered anything. Something that didn't seem important at the time often comes back under pressure. There is a father?''

"Yes, he has a managerial job in the Gas Company. They're prosperous. This is the only child.''

"Has anybody seen the friend who generally walks to school with Clara?''

"They're going round all the children in her class.''

"This girl may not be in her class. She would know if anyone had spoken to Clara on their way. Or they may have had secrets. I'll send Mary Copthorne to talk to her.''

"Yes," Etheridge said. "Or one of the others.''

"Copthorne is much the brightest.''

"All right. Send her. Keep me informed.''

"Of course.''

Back in his own room Corby picked up the blower.

"Is Trent in?''

"He's out on the house-to-house inquiry, Sir.''

"Get my home number, please. And send Detective Constable Copthorne to me.''

His wife answered the telephone at once; he never heard her, even when he was in a hurry, without thinking what a pretty voice it was.

"I don't know when I shall be home. A girl has gone missing.''

His voice sharpened. "Is Tilly in?''

"Yes, she's taken her prep up to her room, and says she doesn't want any supper.''

"She'll change her mind when you have yours.''

"No, she won't. That was Jess. Tilly goes right through punishing herself and other people."

"I haven't time to argue about that now. Goodbye."

Glad to know that Tilly, however supperless and naughty, was safe at home, he gave Mary her instructions, called for his driver and car, and went out after the missing child.

13

SYLVIA CAME INTO the sitting-room with a mug of coffee in her hand.

"Oh, Rodney, I thought you were going out."

"No, I rang the Birketts, and he's in bed with 'flu. I can't think of anybody else I feel like dropping in on."

"I'll get you some coffee."

"I don't want any. Come round to The Feathers with me for half an hour."

"I can't leave Guy alone."

"He's asleep, isn't he?"

"Yes, but he might wake up."

"He never does at this time."

"We can't be certain. He'd be terrified if he found himself alone in the flat."

"He wouldn't be alone in the house. The old bag's never out in the evening. And Ellis is in his room, I heard his radio a few minutes ago. Ask him just to listen for Guy."

"You said he was feeling ill; he's probably gone to bed. No, I can't go. You go."

"I'm sick of going out alone every evening. If it's always going on this way . . . the kid matters and I don't, I'll clear out."

"It isn't that you don't matter, it's just that you're grown up and he isn't. You're his father."

"I never wanted to be."

"But he is your son. Don't you care at all what happens to him?"

"I suppose I do but nothing would happen to him. Why don't you get that woman, Nancy, to come back and baby-sit some evenings?"

"She wouldn't. It's hard enough to get her to stay an extra half-hour in the afternoons."

"Sack her and get someone else."

"Yes, I'm going to."

"You've been going to for a damned long time. The truth is, Sylvia, you're lazy. I know the medics who employ you think you're perfect, but that's because all you have to do is to be nice to people, which is as natural to you as breathing. You've just *got* to have people liking you, and when it comes to making somebody not like you, as it would if you sacked Nancy, you somehow don't do it. The only person you don't mind annoying is me. You are always willing to put the kid first."

Sylvia had an uncomfortable feeling that what he said might be true.

"All right, I'll come . . . for a short time."

"I'll drive you home whenever you like."

"I'll just have a look at Guy first."

"No, you'd wake him. Come along, get your coat, and let's go now. Only for half an hour."

Knowing perfectly well that at the end of half an hour he would feel differently, she shrugged on her coat and ran downstairs after him.

The Three Feathers, the largest and most up-to-date pub in the district, attracted a remarkable variety of customers. East Walburn, like every near-in London suburb, was inhabited by incomers of every race, colour and creed. Rodney cut his way through the crowd, and found a small empty table. It was the kind of thing he never failed to do as Sylvia had noticed with pleasure when she first began to go out with him.

They had met because his firm did accountancy for her three specialists. Neither Sylvia nor Rodney had a flat they thought big enough for two; it was important, Rodney said, to start these things in comfort. Dutton's offer of a short-term lease of a roomy flat just finished came at the right time for them, in fact Sylvia sometimes thought that the only thing that had not gone perfectly for them was Guy.

She had cheated, by not taking the Pill for a few weeks, to get him, and she was not sure that Rodney had ever forgiven her. They still looked now and then at possible houses, but their saving-up was without conviction. They both liked spending money on good clothes, good food and drink, good holidays and a good car. There was no hurry. The unfinished house gave Rodney, as he sometimes recognized, a reassuring feeling of impermanence. Sylvia lately had been less than completely satisfied. She wanted another child.

Rodney came back with their full glasses.

"What a lot of our acquaintances are here tonight, have you noticed? The detective girl is over there by the bar with a prim young man who looks like a policeman off-duty. Or he may be another of the CID keeping an eye on us all in here to see what we get up to. The CID ought to have some kind of uniform too. It's not fair sitting round looking like ordinary people and listening to our criminal conversations."

"You're not planning a crime for tonight, are you?"

"No, not this evening. I've had a busy day. There's Dutton over there with one of his squatters or ex-squatters, a fellow called Gaines."

"I don't know any of them by sight."

"I've run into Gaines once or twice at the petrol station; he's a creep. The other lad who goes about with Gaines is that one in the red jersey on the stool at the end of the bar. I wonder why he's on his own—wants a change perhaps. Dutton and Gaines are probably hatching something."

It was three-quarters of an hour later when Sylvia suddenly looked at her watch.

"Oh, Rodney, I must go. . . . It's nearly ten. Do you mind awfully?"

64

"Take the car. You know where we left it, down at the bottom of Galt Street. I'll get a lift from Dutton."

Ashamed of having forgotten the time, she went out quickly and ran down the long line of parked cars to theirs at the bottom of the side street.

14

CORBY ARRIVED HOME tired and cross in the reaction from anxiety. His wife opened the front door before his key had turned in the lock.

"Is the child found?"

"She is, blast her! She just fancied a day in Peterborough. I'll tell you all about it while we're having supper, or have you had yours?"

"No I waited for you. I'll get it while you have a wash and a drink. Its steak and kidney pudding, and then one of my own cheese-cakes."

He settled himself in his chair by the big gas fire of artificial logs. He had been dubious about it at first as a fake, but he had come to enjoy the glow and liveliness. He often thought, especially at this time of day, how lucky he was in his home. Some of the best pieces of furniture in the room had been inherited from his family or from Lucy's, most of the rest they had bought together, after saving up for them. He had watched Lucy making the curtains for the room, picking up the children's toys from the new carpet they had bought with a small legacy. What was the Arab word, *baraka*, wasn't it, for the deep patina of affection, on a familiar place, which meant comfort and peace?

There was a rift in the peace here; as they sat down he asked for Tilly.

"Hasn't reappeared. I knew she wouldn't. I expect she's in bed and asleep."

"She may be crying her heart out."

"If she is it probably won't be doing her any harm."

"Good God, she's only just thirteen!"

"That's practically grown-up nowadays."

"Said to be but of course it isn't. That's half the trouble with them."

"They think they're entitled to do whatever they feel like. Look at your missing child. She suddenly felt like going to Peterborough so she went, not caring in the least that she was driving her mother half out of her mind, and wasting the time of a busy police station. What they feel like at the moment is their only imperative."

"Perhaps when we were young we didn't get enough of that."

"I should have thought that sort of thing was the cause of two-thirds of your work."

She was probably right, and there was no reason why this should make it all the more irritating. "I suppose you've been out all day chasing that wretched little Clara?"

"No. I didn't hear about it until after five, I'd been out on a bomb hunt. I was sick of reading the reports of them in the office, I thought I'd like to try an afternoon on the fieldwork. I went up to Robin Lane. It runs up the side of the children's playground; do you know it?"

"Yes. Big ugly, empty houses."

"That's right. We had an anonymous letter about them, so I went up with Mary Copthorne and Williams to see if there was anything going on there."

"And there wasn't?"

"I don't think so. I'm not certain. I had a feeling about the letter and the place."

"Your feelings are so often right."

"You mustn't tell me that. I am always telling myself not to trust them too much. By the way I asked Mary Copthorne when she was coming to see us again. I thought she might cheer Tilly up."

"I don't think Tilly is at all interested in her. So far as either of them was her friend it was Jessica. Has Mary Copthorne got the same boy-friend?"

"Robert Prentice. Yes, she has."

"I remember she brought him to one of Jessica's parties. Rather a nice young man, I thought—pleasant and cheerful."

"He seems to me a bit of a chump . . . a very ordinary young man."

"Well, she's a very ordinary girl, isn't she?"

"I wouldn't say that. She's the brightest of our young CID lot. She's got an exceptional zest for the work."

"I wonder how Robert Prentice likes being shacked up with a female detective?"

"Presumably he likes it as he goes on doing it. She's a very charming girl, so good-tempered and willing . . . pretty too."

"Go and sit down. I'll bring coffee."

While she was in the kitchen, he lay back in his big chair and dozed off. In a brief cat-nap he dreamed that he was walking down a familiar road near the place in the country where he grew up. There were tall hedgerows on either side of the road and he was looking in the worried way of some dreams for an opening on one side or the other through which he could get out of it. He woke with a jerk as Lucy came in with two mugs of coffee. She sat down in the chair opposite him and picked up her tapestry frame. She was making seats for their upright chairs. As so often when she was absorbed in something she was doing a lock of hair fell across her cheek, the tip of her tongue showed between her lips. As a young man he had seen this unconscious pose with ecstasy, and still often noticed it with a smile of the heart.

She looked at him holding the needle poised.

"Frank. I'm going to get a job."

"Oh! What kind of job?"

"I think I'll try for something to do with computers. I shall have to get trained for them first."

"Computers! That doesn't sound like you."

67

"People don't have to stay in the same groove all their lives, do they?"

"Of course they don't."

But he had and though there were times when it maddened or depressed him, he seldom wished he had chosen another one, he never really wanted to change. Perhaps Lucy found that dull of him.

"Where would you get this training? How will you find out about it?"

"There's a course at the Tech. in Walburn; It starts on December first. You go from ten to four-thirty five days a week, and it lasts four months."

"Doesn't it stop for the Christmas holidays? The girls will be at home."

"It will break off for Christmas and the girls are quite old enough to look after themselves part of the time."

"How did you find out about it".

"Martin found out for me."

"You've been discussing this with him, have you?"

Martin had been a valued friend of both for several years.

"I was having lunch with him and I just said that I should like to try and get some work outside home."

"Is it because you want to get away from Tilly for a time that you want to do this?"

"Partly, I daresay. She's never at her worst when you're at home. You don't know how trying it is. She's malicious, she sticks pins into me, I don't want to do that to her . . . well, perhaps I do, but I don't think I should let myself. So I want to get another interest outside this house. Most women do now, you know. I guessed you wouldn't like it. You're too old-fashioned."

"Who's sticking pins in now? I should like you to do anything you want to do, anything that makes you happy. I didn't know you weren't. You've always seemed to be."

"Of course I'm happy on the whole. I know very well how lucky I am. But I've begun to realize that when I've had other

68

feelings or wishes I've just thrown them out of my mind, and told myself not to be silly. But now since Mike is mostly away at sea, and the girls are growing up it's different. I can give myself a look-in."

"I shall be very glad if you consider yourself for a change instead of devoting yourself entirely to all of us. Will you have a good chance of getting a job after you've had this computer training."

"Martin thinks so."

Corby restrained himself from saying that he wished Martin had minded his own business.

"Would you be very disappointed if you couldn't get anything?"

"I expect so but then I should try something else. . . . Frank, you're used to women working under you. You always admire them if they're good at their job."

"I do admire anyone who's good at his or her job."

"Mary Copthorne for instance."

"I'm pleased to have someone I recommended to police work doing well in it and enjoying it. But I've always immensely admired you, the way you've done your job, bringing up the children, making such a home for all of us."

"Don't be afraid, I won't make the family or the house suffer because of any other work I do. I've got enough energy for both."

"Lucky girl."

He put out a hand to touch her, but perhaps not seeing it, she folded her tapestry and got up.

"I'm going to bed."

"I'll come soon."

Ruffled, he thought that he had been unreasonable, but felt that Lucy had. He was just going to rouse himself to get the cat in and turn off the heating for the night, when he heard a sound at the door. It opened cautiously, and Tilly came in, wearing a dark anorak over her pale blue pyjamas.

She was rosy from sleep, but her fair head was as smooth as if it had just been brushed.

"Hallo. . . . Why aren't you asleep?"

"I woke up because I'm hungry. I'm going to get something to eat out of the fridge."

"Be quick and bring it back here. You'll get cold with nothing on your feet; why didn't you put your dressing-gown on?"

"This is just as warm."

She vanished into the kitchen and returned a minute or two later, with a glass of milk and a big slice of cheese-cake. She sat down on the floor at his feet.

"You should have a proper supper at the proper time you little goose-girl."

"I didn't feel like it."

"I did. I thought about my supper several times while I was working late, because a silly child who had had a crush on her form mistress went to Peterborough to look for her."

"Peterborough! I wouldn't go across the road to look for my form mistress."

"You know I think it might be nice if you occasionally had some respect for the people who have to teach you."

"I would if they were respectable." They both laughed. "Well, you know what I mean, Dad. But I suppose you have to be on the side of authority."

"Yes. I think a reasonable authority is better than chaos and anarchy."

"Much duller."

"No, I think that's a delusion."

"Did you have some of the cheese-cake or shall I get you a bit?"

"I had some, thanks."

"I do have to say that Mum makes very good ones."

"Tilly! Why can't you get on better with your mother?"

"Because I can't."

"Have you tried?"

"Yes, well—perhaps not very hard lately."

"What's the matter? You must have some idea. You're not a stupid girl."

"I can't really tell you. I've had friends at school that I liked very much, and then after a time some of them, not all, seemed different from what I thought they were, so my liking for them stopped. It's something like that I think."

"But this isn't a passing schoolgirl friendship, it's your *mother*—who has loved you and looked after you ever since you were born."

"I didn't ask her to have me."

"No, I suppose I was responsible for that. You'd better take it out on me."

"I don't want to. You suit me."

"If so perhaps you will oblige me by not making my home so uncomfortable."

"Did you talk to Jessica like that last year when she felt fed up?"

"I really can't remember. I have a lot of people to look after besides my own tiresome children. Now you'd better go to bed. And ease off your antics a bit, will you?"

"Perhaps. I'll see what I can do."

Corby sat back in his chair for the half-hour's read which he generally enjoyed before going to bed. But tonight he could not concentrate. They were all restless, his wife, his daughter, himself. This was no more than natural in two middle-aged people who perhaps needed a change and an adolescent who did not know what she needed. But from the murderous violence about everywhere to children playing truant it seemed to him that most people were trying to jerk themselves out of the situation they were in to try and find another one which might not be there to find.

He remembered how once in the years before capital punishment was abolished, he had had to get some information from a man not much younger than himself who was

71

in a condemned cell. All the time when he was answering the careful questions, the prisoner was walking backwards and forwards, moving his hands, blinking his eyes, kicking the pallet bed as he passed, as if using the power of movement which would so soon be taken away from him. Was the whole world now like that living in a condemned cell, and twitching here, there and everywhere as if to escape the threat?

The child, Clara, had run off to Peterborough to exercise her free-will while she had it. Were the terrorists, the highjackers, the rapists moved disastrously by the same impulse? How could you stop them when the impulse was more dynamic than the wish to contain it? Who in fact would be a policeman? Well, he would. Because it was a job worth doing, and he was trained for it, and recognized in himself a period of flatness and boredom which he had heard about and seen in other people. He smiled as he shut his book and put the lights out. Could that flat time ever come to a young enthusiast like Mary Copthorne? Of course it would if she stayed in the force, but long before she got to that she would be married to Robert Prentice, and bringing up his brats. They lost so many of their best girls that way, and you could not complain, it was natural.

The explosion came when he was halfway up the staircase. The noise seemed to leap through his stomach to his ears. The house shook a little. From outside there was the distant crash of breaking glass. Lucy's bedroom door opened.

"What's that? Was it a bomb?"

"Yes. Probably not so near as it sounded."

He ran down again to the telephone. As he put his hand on the receiver the bell rang. He was aware of Tilly flying across the landing to her mother's room as he pulled on his mackintosh and boots, and hurried out into the night.

15

IN HER OWN flat Rosa switched on the electric fire with which she supplemented the central heating. She loved warmth. She hung her wet cloak over a rail in the bathroom, kicked off her shoes and thankfully pushed her painful feet into her bedroom slippers. In her kitchen she heated some soup and considered making an omelette, but decided that she did not want it enough to make the bother worth while. She buttered a croissant, poured out a glass of wine from the bottle she had opened at midday, put the things on a small tray, and with difficulty carried it back to her sofa.

When she had finished she trailed unevenly across to her writing-desk. Her room was well lit, she loved light as much as she loved warmth, and had a specially strong reading lamp on her desk. She began a letter to her daughter in California. She often wrote to her, often tore up the letters half-finished, when she was overcome by a conviction that Gelsomina would not really want often to hear from her, that she herself, while being careful not to, might have let slip a note of appeal because she did so much want to see, if only once again, her only child. When she and Richard had loved one another so deeply and fully it had always seemed to her that any child of theirs would be born loving, and open-hearted. But Gelsomina was a self-contained creature from the beginning, turning away from caresses. Perhaps she felt that there was no room for her in her parents' complete union.

Rosa's now large handwriting straggled across the page.

"A depressing day of steady rain, falling continuously out of heavy skies. How often in England one longs to put one's hand flat under the sky and push it up! I sometimes wonder, and I expect you do too, why I did not stay on at Le Tavernule, after Adelmo died, especially as I had married him so that I could stay in Tuscany, to try and keep something of my life there, which would always be my real life.

"Adelmo knew it and said that he was prepared to take whatever I could give him, but of course he hoped that I should, as time passed, be able to give him more; I couldn't so he was unhappy and unsatisfied. It was a relief to me when he died and I decided to come here. A flat in this commonplace house, still noisy with builders, and in a mess with their work, is as far as it could be from Le Tavernule, and will do very well for the time I have left.

"A girl police-woman, a detective came to see me today. I expect you will have read that the police are organizing a house-to-house search round London for people who are making IRA bombs or storing the material for them. Someone had written an anonymous letter about this house, a lunatic, I suppose, because I can't see anybody here belonging to the IRA. The girl detective was naïve, pretty in a very English way, and much interested in her work. She looked and sounded happy. Perhaps I am projecting my own feelings when I say that I don't think I see many people who are nowadays.

"But how can they be, when we are all living under the threat of extinction. I am sure you, Gerald, and all your friends must feel this as acutely as we do. Distance makes no difference, and there is no safe place nowadays. People, anyhow the people I see, don't talk very much about it. 'Faces along the bar, cling to their average day.' It is absurd that I should be so conscious of it, because for me personal extinction cannot be far off. I suppose after all I spend less time confronting the nuclear threat because I am so well aware of the personal one. But I do deeply share the general fear, especially for the children. One cannot look at them without longing to snatch them away and somehow save them.

"Well, I must not depress you. I so much enjoyed the photographs of your house. I am glad that Gerald. . . .

She stopped writing and put down her pencil. In the house below she heard a child screaming.

It must of course be Guy, he hardly ever cried at night, or if he did she could not hear him when the doors of both flats were shut. He must have slipped out on to the landing and no doubt in a half-minute Sylvia would come after him and the screaming would stop. But it didn't; Rosa went as quickly as she could to the door and opened it.

The child was on the landing below. Surely they could not have gone out and left him. But evidently they had. She leaned over the bannisters.

Guy's face was scarlet and dripping with tears. It was extraordinary that so small a person could make so much noise. Rosa called out to him.

"Guy! It's all right, darling. What is it? Is your mother not there?"

He stopped screaming for a minute in his surprise at seeing her. His mother must be out, she couldn't have failed to hear that noise.

"Come along darling. Come up to me."

He came up the stairs at a stumbling run, still crying. Rosa put an arm round him and pulled him into her room.

"What is it, Guy? Is Mummy not there?"

"No, there's nobody there."

"I expect she thought you were fast asleep, and perhaps she just went downstairs for a minute."

It did not seem to Rosa herself a very satisfactory explanation.

"But she'll be back very soon. You come and lie down on my sofa by my fire and I'll cover you up. I've got some of the little round chocolates you like, you shall have one, or perhaps even two."

He came and let her roll him up in one of her shawls, and put him comfortably on her sofa; an occasional sob still shook him.

"Where is Mummy?"

"I don't know but she will be back soon. Would you like a chocolate?"

In a faint convalescent voice he murmured "Yes".

"Of course."

A suggestion of a smile just curved his lips, but he asked anxiously.

"Will Mummy know where I am?"

"I'll leave my door open. We shall hear her coming upstairs to your flat, and you can run down."

She gave him the chocolates; he turned on his side, gave a deep sigh, and a minute or two later was asleep. Very carefully she wiped the melted chocolate from round his mouth. She sat quietly by his side looking at him. It pleased her to know that for once she was of use to him. She was getting drowsy herself when she heard a sound in the house below. She struggled on to her feet, and went to the door. She could hear light footsteps below. She opened the door, switched on the staircase light and called.

"Miss Grainger, Miss Grainger."

It softened her heart a little that the face turned up to her was so like Guy's, especially at the moment when the eyes were wide with surprise and alarm.

"Your little boy is here, he's quite all right, I heard him screaming so I brought him to my flat. He's asleep on my sofa."

"Oh that was kind of you! I'm so ashamed! I never do leave him unless there's somebody there. But Rodney so much wanted me to go round to The Feathers with him. Guy never does wake as a rule, it *would* be just the one night when I was out that he did."

Yes, Rosa thought, they have a sixth sense.

"I was very glad that I happened to hear him. You'd better come in and get him."

Sylvia hurried into the room. Rosa followed her more slowly feeling envious of her, glad for the child. As Sylvia gently pulled the shawl away from him, Guy stirred, yawned, opened his eyes, saw his mother, and stretched his arms to her. She lifted him up; he put one arm round her neck, smiled

76

at her; then his head dropped on her shoulder; with another deep sigh he fell asleep again.

Sylvia was renewing her apologies and thanks, when the windows rattled with the loud noise of an explosion.

"What was that? A car backfiring I suppose."

"No, I don't think so. I think it was a bomb."

"A bomb. But why? It sounded as if it was just outside the house."

"I think it was further off than that."

"Oh! Could it have been as far as The Feathers? I hope Rodney is all right. Are you quite sure it wasn't a car?"

Rosa was but there seemed no point in saying so.

"I shouldn't worry if I were you, I should go and put Guy to bed."

"Yes, I'd better. Are you all right alone up here?"

"Oh, I shall be quite all right."

"I'll leave you in peace, then. Goodnight, and thank you again."

"Goodnight."

Rosa watched the young woman carefully carrying the child downstairs and in at the doorway below. She went across to her desk, picked up her half-written letter to her daughter, tore it across and threw the fragments into the wastepaper basket. She began the slow process of getting ready for bed.

Sylvia's was not an anxious nature. After she had put Guy back to bed she sat reading for half an hour, waiting for Rodney to come home or to ring up and let her know if he was all right—if it really was a bomb, which now that she was away from Rosa's conviction began to seem to her very doubtful. After a time she fell asleep. She did not know for how long but she was awakened by the sound of a key turning in the front door.

Rodney came in.

"Asleep?"

"I have been, but I'm awake now. What time is it?"

"After midnight. Didn't you hear the bomb?"

"Mrs Spinelli said it was one. But I didn't know. Where was it?"

"In a car parked in Galt Street, you know, down the side of The Three Feathers."

Sylvia was wide awake now.

"But it must have been very near you!"

"It was."

"Was anybody hurt?"

"Two people in the house opposite where the car was parked were hurt, I don't know how badly. They were taken off to hospital. The blast broke down the wall of the kitchen at the back of The Feathers, and there was a lot of broken glass, people cut and suffering from shock. I gather the police thought it was a failure from the point of view of the bombers who had it in the car. Which of course was smashed to bits and the one next to it was on fire. But on the whole we were lucky. I feel half-deafened by the noise. We had to stay there such a long time while the police got all our names and addresses. I hope you weren't worried. But I suppose you found Guy safe in bed so you weren't."

"I didn't know what it was or where it was. Guy was with Mrs Spinelli, she heard him crying."

"I told you he wasn't alone in the house, so he'd be all right.

"I'm not surprised that girl came about bombs this afternoon. It looks as if there was something going on in this district. Well, go to sleep again. I'm going to have a bath. I shan't sleep if I go to bed now. Goodnight."

16

BACK IN HIS own room, Dutton sank into an easy chair, picked up the telephone and dialled a Bradford number. A drowsy voice answered him. "Yes?"

"Mabel, it's Sam."

"Aye. I thought it must be."

"I wanted you to know that I am safe, before you heard the news."

"What have you been doing to get into the news?"

"Nothing . . . I was in The Three Feathers this evening and a bomb hidden in a parked car outside went off. It broke all the windows and brought a bit of the kitchen wall down."

"Eh, there's no end to it! Was anyone killed?"

"No, there were people hurt and cut with glass, and some had to be treated for shock. I didn't want you to hear about it before I spoke to you. I was afraid you'd get worrying about me."

"I don't know that I should. I reckon you'd always be one of those that turned up alive. But I'm glad it was no worse. What was the sense of letting off a bomb there?"

"I don't think it was meant to go off there. I don't know whether the IRA have claimed it. The police kept us there a damned long time taking our names and addresses."

"They've got their job to do."

"I'm not saying they haven't. But I was in a hurry to get home to speak to you, so that if it was on the radio you wouldn't be frightened."

"I shouldn't have been listening to the radio while tomorrow morning."

The conversation was not going as Dutton thought it should. Mabel did not really seem to be much disturbed by learning of the danger he had so narrowly escaped.

"If you've nothing else to say, Sam, I'd like to get to sleep. I think I've got a cold coming on so I took myself to bed with a hot drink."

"I'm sorry to have disturbed you. But I did want to ask you just once again. . . .

"No."

"No what?"

79

"I'm not going to sell this house. We've got to have a roof over our heads."

"If you'd sell the house or even let it we should have a roof over our heads down here. A nice flat would mean much less work for you, and we'd have good money coming in from the other flats."

"And all the bother of things going wrong in the other flats, and the tenants complaining, and their children screaming, and all their visitors tramping downstairs after midnight shouting goodbye. No, people of our age want to live in a house of their own, and near their old friends. They don't want to move to a great city full of strangers."

"There are so many more opportunities down here."

"You're better off without opportunities. We're still paying after the last one. No, this is a right comfortable house in good order and I'm going to stay here. Now get yourself a night-cap, and go to bed and get some sleep. I daresay the bomb gave you a shake-up. You'd better come up here for the weekend. We've not had the IRA yet in Bradford."

In a desperate attempt to bring her to a more caring state of mind, he said, "We've had the police here today, looking for bombs or explosives in this house."

"Well, they weren't far out, were they, if there was a bomb as near as The Feathers. I don't suppose they found anything in your place?"

"Of course they didn't find anything. My tenants are all very respectable people."

"Even respectable people do some funny things nowadays. But I want to get to sleep, Sam. Let me know if you're coming up Saturday. I shan't bother with a joint for Sunday if you're not. A nice pork chop will do for me. Goodnight."

PART THREE

17

ROBERT PRENTICE WOKE in the morning with a slight
headache and a queasy stomach, both of which he was
unaccustomed to. It did not occur to him that a bomb going
off the night before outside the pub in which he was sitting
could have given him a shock. That kind of thing naturally
gave women a shock. He had been sorry for one or two girls at
the bar who had screamed, and for an older woman who had
fainted. He supposed that he himself had woken up feeling
off-colour, because he had had a couple of extra pints while
they were all waiting for the police to let them go.

He did not even know that he would have been more
pleased with Mary if she had screamed or fainted, instead of
at once going to the telephone that stood on the bar and
ringing the police station. Then she showed her card to the
landlord and asked him to prevent anyone from going out to
see what had happened until the police came, which they did
in three or four minutes. Mary came back to their table,
picked up her glass without sitting down, finished her drink;
she left Robert saying that she would be wanted. She was but
he wasn't, though he offered to help, but he only found himself
listening interminably to a fat old man who had taken part in
the D-Day landing, and wanted to tell somebody what it was
like being under shell-fire.

Robert, like all except those who were suffering from cuts
or shock, had to stay until his name and address had been
taken. It was no use attempting to see Mary again. He went

home to a restless night, and was now sitting in his room at the office, going through his paper work, and dictating his letters. His mind was on his work, he had trained himself to that and was interested in it, but this morning he felt an undertow of flurry and disappointment. He wished it was his day for outside work; he took the firm's car and visited some of the branches and customers in the further-out suburbs on one day a week.

He knew that he did his job well, but he was so far below par this morning that when he was summoned to the room of Mr Shepperton, the Managing Director, he wondered if he had made a bloomer.

But he had not been summoned for anything like that; it was for promotion.

"It's pretty good, isn't it Mary?"

She hugged him again.

"It's perfectly splendid, Robbie. I'm delighted. I do congratulate you."

"Old Fawcett doesn't want to do the outside work any longer. In fact he's going to retire before next summer. I shall be going round the other branches and the customers four days a week, and just have one day in the office to write my reports, and to see that my calls are followed up."

"And you like the outside work so much."

"I do and they're getting a new car for me, and I can use it for my own purposes at the weekends so long as I pay for my petrol, and bring it in cleaned and polished on Monday morning."

They were sitting side by side on the window-seat in Mary's little sitting-room. On the table lay a bunch of shop roses in a tube of cellophane. Mary picked up the flowers.

"I must put them in water straight away. I wish I'd got something special for dinner. It's only a bought quiche and salad and cheese. I didn't have time today to make anything."

"Never mind. We can have a quiet evening and discuss plans. Do you realize the difference this will make to us? We can get a mortgage on a flat or on a small house. We'll start looking round."

"I've got awfully fond of this little flat."

"Yes, but it would be cramping for two people to live in. We can afford something better now."

In the middle of his own exaltation he became aware that she was not quite so excited as he would have expected. He looked at her closely and saw that she was pale and had dark rings under her eyes.

"Did you sleep last night?"

"Not much. Did you?"

"Not for some time."

"I was very tired. I kept going off and then waking up with a jerk. I suppose having a bomb drop so near you and people hurt is a shock."

Her saying that was a relief to him. It made her seem more feminine and vulnerable. He put an arm round her and hugged her to him.

"But they were pleased with me for getting on to the station quickly. I'm always so glad when I've done the right thing. Corby, my father's old friend, you know, who got me into the police, was pleased with me."

"You'd have got into the police anyhow."

"I might have but I'm grateful all the same, and glad when he thinks I've done well. I admire him so much. He's just what I think a policeman ought to be."

"My Pakistani friends don't like the police much. They say they're rough and hard on ethnic minorities."

"That's a cliché. They've heard it on TV or radio, and not understood that there's another side to it."

"I daresay they have friends with reason to complain of the police."

"Have any policemen really treated your Paki friends badly."

"I haven't heard of it."

"And you? Have any policemen ever been rough with you or treated you badly?"

Robert, who was privately thinking that she had been more upset by the bomb than she knew, had the sense to laugh and reply,

"None of them except you."

Mary laughed too and the cloud that had begun to spread over their sky receded. They started to get supper ready, and to discuss where they should go out to dinner for their celebration.

18

I SENT FOR you, Sister Catherine," the Mother Superior said, "because I think the time has come to make a change in your work".

The young nun looked startled. She seemed to be about to speak, but lowered her eyelids so that her long dark lashes rested on her cheeks.

"I think you understood when you received the grace of a vocation that it would entail sacrifices of all kinds."

"Yes, Reverend Mother."

"In the religious life sacrifices are not always what one expects them to be. It is sometimes easier to make willingly the large sacrifices for which one has prepared oneself than the smaller ones for which one may not be prepared. You understand that?"

"Yes, Reverend Mother."

"You made most freely and generously the first great sacrifice. You left your life in the world—and for the young, especially, it can be a very pleasant world, with many opportunities of serving God in it. But you relinquished it. You left your home, your family, your father and mother and your two brothers. Yes? Did you want to say something?"

"Only one brother now, Reverend Mother."

"I know. I do not forget to pray for the soul of your elder brother as I am sure all the sisters do. At the time of which I am speaking he was alive. But," she smiled faintly "the sacrifice that I am asking of you is nothing to do with your family. It is to do with your work, I am arranging for you to give up your work with the laundry, anyhow for the time being."

"Oh no!"

The exclamation broke involuntarily from the girl's lips. She pressed them together as if she wanted to prevent them from letting any more out.

The Mother Superior laughed. "*Mais oui*. Oh, yes! You see how necessary it is that you should make the change. A nun must always be detached. Her attachment is to God, to His Holy Church, and to her Order. You have allowed yourself to become a little too much attached to the laundry work, too personally involved. It is right, of course, to put a good deal of yourself into any work you do, but not too much. So I am going to transfer you to work in the garden."

"In the garden," the girl repeated. She sounded like somebody in shock.

"Yes. You are one of the youngest of us. Gardening is hard work. Do not look so sad. I can well understand that to go driving about the town, and dealing with people in the outside world is more enjoyable than thrusting a spade into this heavy clay soil. Perhaps it may only be for a time. We shall see."

"I have been most careful, Reverend Mother, in all my dealings with our customers. I have kept a list of the times at which it is convenient for each one that I should call. I have been careful to keep exactly to those times because if I am late and they are waiting to take in their laundry before they go out, they may lose patience and may change to another laundry."

"I know that you have been most practical and conscientious. Your list will be very useful to Sister **Maria** who will take over the laundry work. You will go round with her in the van for the first week, so that she can learn your good ways. After that Sister Veronica will tell you exactly what she wants you to do in the garden.

"I shall make a special intention for you at Mass on the day when you begin the new work, and I shall look forward to seeing the most beautiful flowers on the chapel altar very soon."

19

THE KITCHEN AT Greenways was the warmest room in the house, but also the most dilapidated. A great deal of the paint that had been applied to it when the house was inhabited had long ago worn off. The linoleum, laid probably at the same time, had become a mass of dangerous holes and worn patches. The gas stove was so old that it resisted all efforts to clean it. In spite of these drawbacks the three ex-squatters had their meals in the kitchen because it was not worth the trouble of carrying them into a much colder room.

Breakfast varied according to the housekeeping funds. If they were in pretty good shape, Truda and Toby had eggs and bacon or sausages. If the housekeeping funds were low, they had fried bread, which was at least hot, and could, with a dash of chutney or of tomato sauce, be made quite tasty. Shelton had coffee and toast taken up to him in his bedroom, generally by Truda, who was pleased if she got a smile or a word of thanks from him at the beginning of her day.

She was not one of those people who remain sleepy for some time after getting up. She would have liked to talk to Toby during breakfast, he was generally an easy companion, but at breakfast he insisted on silence. This was, he explained to Truda, because it was during the night that he was in closest touch with his unconscious mind, and it was from his unconscious that he got his inspiration. The first hour in the morning was the time when it might be expected to give him an idea for a poem, if not a few lines. He needed quiet in which to receive them. He always had a notebook and pencil by his coffee cup. Now and then Truda slipped another slice of fried bread on to his plate, or refilled his cup with Nescafé. She could not read the paper even if she had been in the habit of reading newspapers, Shelton always had it upstairs. If she looked out of the window she could only see a mass of dingy evergreens in the neglected garden. It was very dull for her.

This morning after the excitement of hearing the bomb last night she could not keep quiet.

"Toby, do you think that the policeman who came yesterday knew that a bomb was probably going to explode somewhere near here?"

"I shouldn't think so or he would have warned everybody."

"But the person who wrote the anonymous letter, might not know exactly where it would be."

"No I suppose not."

Toby rubbed his eyes.

"Did you have a good night?"

She meant, "Was your unconscious helpful?"

"No, I couldn't sleep. It was the bomb I think. My head ached for a long time after the noise, and all the fuss afterwards. I don't feel like writing this morning. I haven't written a decent line this week."

"But you did last week. You were pleased with the poem you wrote."

"It's not as good as I thought it was. Is there any marmalade?"

"No, I couldn't afford it. There's hardly any money left. Shall I do you another slice of fried bread?"

"No thanks. We've had it three mornings in the last week. There ought to be some money left, surely."

"I'm very careful, Toby. I write down whatever I spend.

You could look at it but you always say you can't be bothered."

"Oh, I know you're careful, it isn't that I don't trust you, of course I do. It's Shelton I don't trust."

This remark so astonished Truda that she opened her mouth but said nothing.

"It's not long since I gave him the money for a new copy of the magazine, and some housekeeping. But no magazine, and nothing but bloody fried bread."

"There are a few biscuits in the tin."

"Oh, don't be a fool, Truda. Can't you see there's something wrong?"

"I expect Shelton can explain. Why don't you ask him?"

Toby hadn't asked because he was afraid of Shelton, and also felt a certain delicacy about calling him to account for money that he had handed over to him.

"You see my mother sends money for the magazine and naturally she wants to know why it doesn't come out. Even that policeman noticed that the last number was dated June. I *need* the magazine because I want to have printed copies of my poems to show to people, to editors and publishers. I have to wait and wait. . . ."

"Couldn't you get some of your poems published in other magazines?"

This was a question which Toby preferred not to be asked.

Truda said kindly, "You're only quite young. I'm sure you'll get a whole lot of your poems published in time."

"In time . . . in time . . . but we don't know how much time we've got. Time means something quite different nowadays . . . Truda! Don't talk to me, *please*."

He had snatched his notebook towards him, and hunched himself over it. It looked as though his unconscious had after all come up to scratch. Truda went softly round the table to remove his plate and mug. She stacked but did not wash up, because the noise of the water might disturb him. She slipped out of the room and went upstairs to make beds. When she came down again she saw that there was quite a lot of writing on the pad. Toby was leaning back in his chair, wearing a look of rainwashed calm.

"Would it run to another cup of coffee?"

She shook the Nescafé jar over his mug.

"Just."

As she threw the empty coffee jar in the rubbish-bin she muttered to herself, "We shall *have* to have some money."

"I've got some upstairs, I'll give you some. Don't bother me now. I haven't quite finished, and I think I need to rewrite the first three lines."

Toby brooded over the poem, then suddenly added a few lines, and sat back in his chair shining with relief.

"I'm glad you've finished it before you have to go out."

"I don't have to go out."

"But you nearly always do."

"I go to oblige Shelton. But after all it's my car."

It had never occurred to her to wonder where they went to, or what they did. They always seemed to her to be creatures out of another world. But Toby had never talked to her so much before. She knew that they were all three registered as unemployed, and drew social security. She was puzzled.

"But you and Shelton don't work. Except, I mean, for your poetry."

"I don't know what Shelton does."

"But you both go together."

"We start together, but he drops me at the London Library or somewhere. Then he takes the car on, and picks me up towards the end of the afternoon. I read or write in the library, and I go and try to see editors or publishers, or I meet a friend or something. But I don't know where Shelton goes nor what he does. It's odd when you come to think of it."

"Couldn't you ask him?"

"I don't, somehow."

"Are you a little bit afraid of him?"

"Yes, I suppose so, and you are too . . . more than a little."

"I'm always afraid of anybody I like."

"Are you? Why?"

"I'm afraid they might stop liking me."

It was Toby's private opinion that Shelton had never started liking her. He never considered her nor showed her any kindness.

"Are you afraid of me, Truda?"

She considered seriously.

"A little, perhaps. Not much. But I do like you, it's different."

"Truda! Why don't you leave here and get a decent job? With people who pay you?"

"I couldn't. There aren't any jobs."

"Yes, there are, I think, for someone who can shop and clean and cook, and do that sort of thing."

"I don't want to work for just anybody."

"You could probably choose."

She did not want to say to him that people who were not Shelton were just anybody. She had been given so many new ideas this morning that she wanted to be left alone to think about them. "I'm going to wash the kitchen floor now."

That generally got rid of them.

Shelton came in at that moment, carrying the paper in one hand and his radio in the other.

He said to Toby, "That bomb wasn't meant to go off near the Feathers last night. The timing device went wrong. The IRA have rung up the Press to say that it was meant to destroy a well-known public figure, and that the next one will not fail."

"It looks as though that policeman was on the track of something but he hadn't got it right. Truda wants to wash the floor now, Shelton, and she wants some housekeeping money."

"Well, I haven't got any."

Shelton sounded completely indifferent.

To his surprise, and to Toby's, Toby said, "Is that because

92

you've paid the printers for the June number of *Explosion*?"

"I'll tell you in the car; we are going out, I suppose?"

"If you like. We'd better get out of Truda's way anyhow."

Truda fetched the bucket and deck-scrub out of the scullery, and stood looking at the floor. Toby ran in again and held out a five pound note to her.

"That'll do for some food to go on with. We must have a more definite arrangement."

Truda heard the car going down the drive. She had the house to herself now, which by daylight she liked, but after standing about thinking vaguely for a few minutes, she took the bucket and scrub back to the scullery. She decided to wash up quickly, and go out to the shops. She just might go in to the only local café there and have another cup of coffee and even a cake. She was still hungry. For the first time since she had been living at Greenways, she had begun to feel that she had wishes of her own, and that it would not be unthinkable occasionally to gratify them.

20

MERVYN ELLIS RAKED together a pile of the clotted wet leaves covering the middle path, wearily lifted up his two boards, and hoisted his load on to the barrow which he reluctantly saw would not take any more without the bother of wheeling it down to the bottom of the garden and emptying it—and then the whole thing to do over again. And when, he would like to know, was he going to be paid for it all?

As he tipped his load on top of the heap, he noticed that his opposite number next door had come out of the convent, and was starting on the same job. He also saw that she did not like it any more than he did. She raked the leaves together as if she was punishing them for needing it. She hurled them on to her heap, and banged them down on top with her fork as if she was killing them. Mervyn had seen her gardening several times, and had thought how much he would like to speak to her. They were both young, they were fellow sufferers, but he was sure she was not allowed to speak to a man. Always ready to imagine the worst, he was afraid that, if he spoke to the girl, the nuns might make trouble for him with Dutton, and he would lose his job, such as it was. He could easily picture her complaining indignantly to the head of the convent, and her complaining to Dutton, so that he would lose the feeling of occupation, and the hope however slender, of some payment.

All the same he kept on looking at the girl as she worked. She was a companion in misfortune. She was also, even in the long black overall and beret which the convent permitted for gardening, very pretty.

So was the afternoon. The sky was a clear, pale blue with only a few small clouds in the west, where the sun showed promise of going down in splendour before long. Everyone in the district was burning leaves, swirls of blue-grey smoke came across with the smell of bonfires.

Mervyn decided that he had done enough for one afternoon. His leaves were wet, but he would put a light to the heap and anyhow get them started. He had provided himself with a couple of firelighters. He pushed them underneath, and put a match to them.

As he straightened his back he saw that the nun too had decided to call it a day. He also saw that she had piled her heap of leaves close to the uneven beech hedge which divided the two gardens; it was very much too near to the neat little wooden tool-shed, which, Mr Dutton had told him, friends of the convent had presented to it on Sister Veronica's seventieth birthday.

He looked at his own bonfire, which in spite of the firelighters showed every sign of going out. He didn't suppose that the nun would do much harm, he himself would need far more fire-lighters, a whole packet, which he supposed he would have to pay for. He was sure the nun wouldn't have any. Really if she was going to be their regular gardener, they might show her a few things.

But if she had no fire-lighters she had something else. He saw her stoop to pick up a tin. She hurled a stream of petrol on to the fire. A blaze shot up, evidently much higher than she had expected, for perhaps in panic rather than with any purpose she threw the tin on to the heat. Petrol ran out of it, one section of the beech hedge crackled and shot off sparks. A flame reached the roof of the tool-shed and licked across it. The nun with a shriek backed away from what she had done and looked despairingly towards the convent, where no face showed in any of the windows.

Mervyn pushed through a weak place in the hedge, and thrust his fork into the fire. He threw a load of burning leaves on to the path. He reached up and banged out the flames creeping across the roof of the tool-shed. Fortunately for him the leaves were all so wet that even petrol would probably not have destroyed the damp tool-shed in the end. It was the hedge that Mervyn really minded about. Little as he liked the garden or the work in it the alarm roused something in him ready to defend his own territory. In a few minutes there was nothing left of the fire but blackened leaves and smoke. Mervyn had been frightened and said angrily to the nun,

"For heaven's sake be careful. Don't use petrol without knowing what you're doing. You nearly burnt the hedge."

He stood there for a moment half-expecting her to thank him, but she was still angry. She picked up the fork which she had let fall and jabbed it fiercely into the ground. She grasped the skirts of her overall, and her feet in their flat-soled shoes kicked up behind as she ran up the path and in the back door of what had once been the stable yard.

Mervyn turned away towards his own tool-shed. The bad-tempered bitch might just have said "Thank you."

But the angry girl was honest, or the rules of confession were too strict to be evaded. A day or two later, Mervyn received a note, very neatly typed on convent-headed paper, and signed "Jeanne, *Mère Supérieure*." She thanked him for his help to "our gardener who is not yet very experienced".

Mervyn kept the note with a vague idea of showing Dutton one day that *some* people appreciated him.

21

THE DINNER TO celebrate Robert's promotion started well. He had chosen an Italian Restaurant in St John's Wood, a more expensive restaurant than either of them had ever been to but not so grand as to be daunting. Mary had washed her hair the night before; she had put on her suede trousers, and her frilled shirt.

They read the menu from cover to cover over a leisurely drink, and chose at Robert's insistence without considering the price. He ordered with a wordly air, "a bottle of your red house wine". He had once heard Mr Shepperton remark to a customer that this was always the safest bet. The restaurant had no house wine, but they were adaptable. The waiter produced a bottle of average Chianti, and said that most of their customers preferred their house wine to all others.

It was one of those Italian restaurants where the waiters run about all the time with a great air of willingness, and make far more noise with their conversation than the customers, almost enough noise to drown the canned music gushing from the walls.

"This is a *lovely* place," Mary said.

"Yes, it's not a bad little bistro," Robert agreed negligently.

Wine, food and noise went pleasantly to their heads. They laughed a good deal at their own witty remarks and at each other's. Robert felt especially happy. He had been aware lately of a sort of near-flatness in their meetings. Tonight his own pretty girl laughing and chattering so happily opposite to him was, more then he knew, a relief to his mind. With the coffee they become quieter, replete, a little tired by the noise and by their own high spirits.

"Will you have a liqueur, Mary? A cherry brandy or something?"

"What are those people having over there? Do look. It's on fire on their glasses, but it doesn't seem to crack them. Look, that table near the door."

Robert glanced over his shoulder.

"I don't know what it is?"

"It's fascinating. A sort of magic. Do ask the waiter what it is."

"I don't think we need to know, do we?"

"Yes, I do."

"I'm going to order two cherry brandies."

When the waiter came up with the brandies, Mary inquired,

"Do tell me, what is that drink that looks on fire but doesn't burn the glasses."

"Sambuca, Signorina." To Robert he said: "The Signorina wishes to try some? You permit me to offer a little glass on the house?"

"No, thank you."

With an inward shrug at this ungallant Englishman, the waiter withdrew.

"Why did you have to ask him, Mary?"

"Because I wanted to know. If I want to know anything I like to find out. I suppose that's why I'm so glad to be made a detective."

"I should have thought it was far more useful and interesting to be an ordinary police-woman."

"No, it isn't. That was interesting too. I enjoyed it. But it's not quite *so* interesting."

"A lot of what you have to look into must be pretty squalid."

"Yes it is, but that doesn't mean it isn't interesting too."

"For a woman I should have thought it would."

"You mean you think it ought to be, women ought not to want to look into squalor?"

That was exactly what Robert had meant.

"Well I think it must be more trying for them than for men."

"If they all felt like that there wouldn't be any police-women at all."

"Would that matter much?"

"Of course it would. They've got a good deal to contribute to the Force."

"The world had gone on for a good many years without them."

"So it had without electricity."

There was no obvious answer to this. Robert shifted his ground.

"I don't suppose you would ever have thought of being a police-woman if your father's old friend hadn't pressurized you into it."

"I don't know. I might have thought of it, but perhaps I shouldn't have gone in to it without him. I've always been very grateful to him."

"I know you have, damn his eyes."

"Robert, please don't spoil this lovely evening."

"I'm not spoiling it."

"Who is then? It seems to be getting spoilt."

"Oh Mary, what's the matter? You never used to be like this. It's all because of our unsettled life."

"Is it unsettled?"

"Of course it is. We love each other but we don't live together. We often have to postpone our meetings because of your work. If you want to work of course I wouldn't try to prevent you, but if you had a job with ordinary hours like mine and you were not being called on for emergencies, we could be peaceful. I want us now to have a home of our own. I won't mind whether we get a mortgage on a small house or flat, whichever you would like better."

"I don't really want to move just now."

"Why not just now?"

"Because I want to get really run in to the CID work. I don't want to move until I have a lot of time and thought to give to settling into a house or a flat. There are always so many things to do in a new place."

"But I should do a lot of them. We could deal with them together in our weekends and so on. But that's not really the point. I want to marry you, Mary. I love you and I'm sick of only having half of you. Will you marry me?"

"Oh, Robert, I don't want to just yet."

"Why not? We could be very happy together."

"We are now."

"Not nearly as happy as we could be. The way we go on isn't real, it isn't solid, it's dodging the risks."

"What risks?"

"The risks that we might not make a go of it. I know it's easier to get out of it now than it used to be. But it seems to me it's generally a mess all the same."

"I don't want to marry, not just now. I think I'm frightened of ties."

"No, you're not. You're tied to the police force."

"I can throw off that tie whenever I like."

"Do, then. Throw it off now."

"I don't want to."

"Don't you see that if you love somebody you want to be tied to him?"

"I think we're different, you and I."

"Of course we're different. Do you want to marry a twin?"

"I don't want to marry anybody. Not just now."

"Don't you want children?"

"I'm sure I shall sometime."

"You're twenty-eight now. You'll be thirty before you know. That's not young for beginning to have babies."

"Robert, do let me alone!"

"Do you mean that?"

"Yes. I do."

"All right then, I'll take you home now, and after that I'll let you alone."

"Just as you like."

"It isn't what I like, any of it, it's what you like, you want your own way all the time."

"So do you. Doesn't everybody?"

Robert gestured so sternly that their waiter broke off a most interesting conversation with one of his colleagues, and glided smiling to their table.

"The bill please."

The waiter said, "I hope everything has been okay? I hope the Signorina has enjoyed her dinner."

"Oh, yes, she's enjoyed it."

Putting down his credit card and a tip he thought what a lot of money it was when everything had gone wrong at the end.

They did not speak on the short drive home, until in a street lined on both sides with parked cars. Robert, usually a most sensible driver, just missed a woman who stepped recklessly from between two cars.

"Oh, be careful," Mary exclaimed before she knew she was going to.

He accelerated without answering. She kept quiet, and in a minute or two he dropped to his ordinary speed. When they arrived at her door she thanked him warmly. "Such a nice cheerful place, and the most delicious dinner." She added diffidently. "Won't you come in?"

"No thanks. I'm tired."

"Goodnight, then."

"Night."

He drove off.

She went upstairs to her flat and saw on the table in the sitting-room, the tray with tea things, and a tin of Robert's

100

favourite biscuits. She pushed the tray away from her with such violence that it skidded over the edge of the table, to the floor. One cup was broken, the tea-bags in the open packet scattered tea dust all over the floor. Without bothering to pick anything up, she threw herself into one of the chairs, and began to cry, gulping like a child, and with tears running down her cheeks.

2

ON HER WAY home from work Sylvia usually stood on the elevator at Green Cross tube station. She liked the sensation of being lifted to the upper air, but this evening she ran up the other side of the long staircase because she had been kept late in Harley Street, and she never felt sure that she could trust Nancy not to go and leave Guy alone.

Nancy had not gone. Sylvia could hear her speaking to Guy in the edgy voice that always made her decide to get someone else, although somehow she had not yet done it.

Nancy had probably heard her coming for she finished her sentence to the child with the would-be agreeable, "That's a good little boy, then," which always sounded false. Sylvia ran up the last few steps.

"I'm sorry I'm so late. We had a crisis in Harley Street, one of the electric circuits in the house fused, and I had to stay until the emergency electric people came. It was kind of you to wait."

"I waited because I wanted to have a word with you, Miss Grainger."

Sylvia knew that it would be a word that she did not want to hear. When she was in a good temper, Nancy always awarded her an honorary Mrs Landon.

"I'm leaving this job. It's not doing my arthritis any good standing outside that school in the cold. And then it's quite a

101

walk there and back, and I can't wear boots because of my varicose veins. And Guy is always so troublesome when I get him home.''

"He's tired," Sylvia thought, "and you rub him up the wrong way."

"You won't be coming after this week, then?''

"I shan't be coming after today, Miss Grainger.''

"Very well, I'll give you your money for this week. It would be convenient if you could do tomorrow for me.''

"I'm too tired to do another day.''

Sylvia, too much annoyed to speak, fished her wallet out of her bag and handed over the notes. With these in her hand Nancy attempted a more affable farewell.

"I hope you'll soon suit yourself, Mrs Landon, and find somebody else. Goodbye, Guy, I shan't be fetching you from school any longer.''

Guy, who was kneeling on the floor fitting some pieces of Leggo together did not answer. Sylvia admonished him automatically. "Say goodbye to Nancy, Guy.''

"Goodbye.''

Frowning, he pulled a bright coloured shaft out of what was clearly proving to be the wrong place.

Nancy snorted, "Some children have such sweet little ways.''

When she had left, Sylvia snatched up Guy and danced round the room with him in her arms.

"There now. She's gone. And now where am I going to find somebody to look after you?''

"You can look after me.''

He clasped her arms round her knees, and pressed his face against her corduroy trousers.

"I've got to work.''

"Why?''

"To earn some money for us.''

"Dad does that.''

"Yes, but we want some more. How could we buy all this

102

Leggo? Never mind, you shall have some tea now. I'll just fetch the milk, I forgot to bring it up.''

On the stairs she met Mervyn Ellis. He had obviously been gardening. His hands were caked with mud, his boots squelched water.

"Oh, you do look wet and cold! Why don't you come and have a cup of tea with Guy and me?"

Mervyn accepted with such obvious surprise and pleasure that she wondered vaguely why they didn't ask him in oftener, although she knew the answer really. Rodney wouldn't put up with him.

Mervyn came back cleaner, and they made hot buttered toast and spread it thickly with jam.

"You must have been gardening in the dark; how do you manage?"

"I've got a lantern down there."

"But it must be miserable; do you need to go on so late?"

An idea flashed across her mind. "I suppose you wouldn't like a very small temporary job at the end of the afternoon?"

"There isn't much at the Job Centre this time of year."

"I wasn't thinking of the Job Centre. How would you like to fetch Guy back from school at four for a few afternoons? Just till I find someone instead of Nancy, she isn't coming any more. We didn't like her much, did we Guy?"

"She smacked me. She smacked me hard because I pushed her when she was going to tread on my fire engine."

Sylvia said with a complete lack of conviction,

"I suppose you shouldn't have pushed her. What about it, Mervyn?"

Mervyn was thinking. The last part of the afternoon when it was beginning to grow dark was his time for getting on with his special private job.

"Of course I should pay you the same as I paid Nancy. She had fifteen pounds a week."

Mervyn was very short of money, saving all he could for his

private purpose, but an even stronger pressure than that was that he was constitutionally incapable of saying "No" when he was asked to oblige anybody.

"If you could just do it for a few days," Sylvia pleaded.

"Just till I find someone. I'll telephone the Registry in the morning, I promise I will. But it's difficult for me to see anyone except at the weekends. Couldn't you just help me out? It would be so much nicer to have someone we know, wouldn't it, Guy?"

Guy gave Mervyn an examining look but made no comment.

Mervyn felt almost as if he was being asked to take charge of an animal out of the zoo, but his voice said,

"Well, I will until you find someone."

"Oh, isn't that nice! Isn't it kind of Mervyn, Guy? He's going to fetch you back from school tomorrow."

"But *you'll* come home to tea, Mummy?"

"Yes, or course, darling."

Guy nodded satisfied.

23

IN HIS OWN flat upstairs Mervyn had one of his shaking fits of rage. Why did everybody expect him to do things for them? Why did nobody realize that he had affairs of his own quite as important as theirs? Far more important! They were so stupid that they couldn't understand what mattered most now. And why did he always say "yes" when he was asked to do anything?—as if he was an automatic machine, and anybody had only to press a lever.

He would stop it. He would begin now. He would go upstairs, and tell Sylvia that on thinking it over he couldn't spare the time to fetch her blasted kid home from school. It wasn't worth bothering about him, because that kid would never live to grow up unless his parents realized what was happening in the world, and did something to protect him . . . if you could. . . .

Mervyn sat down on his bed suddenly exhausted. There was a knock at the door; he roused himself to open it. Sylvia stood there, a bright-coloured apron over her working suit, her hair ruffled by a cushion fight with Guy.

"I'm so sorry to disturb you. I've just realized that you don't know where Guy's school is. We take him there in the car every morning on our way to work. If you could bear to come with us tomorrow morning, we'd start ten minutes earlier then usual, and come back and drop you here before we go to our jobs. Would 9.20 be possible for you?

"Quite all right, thank you."

"It is good of you. We'll meet downstairs then tomorrow morning. Could you be down at 9.15 perhaps? That would give us a bit more time."

"Yes, I will."

"Bye then. See you. Good night."

They always won in the end.

Mervyn was indignant again, and also frightened when he set out next day to fetch Guy. Since he left school where he had been very much a loner, he had hardly had anything to do with children. How was he to control this one whom he often heard yelling out protests on the landing below him? Suppose the wretched kid suddenly dashed out into the middle of the road and got run over? Suppose it rained, would he be expected to hold an umbrella over his charge? He hadn't got one. What was the use of having an umbrella? "Something is going to fall like rain, and it won't be flowers." Who had written that, Auden wasn't it? He had seen it printed at the beginning of a book on nuclear weapons and it had stayed in his mind.

One small comfort was that it was not raining. It was a fine November afternoon with the last red and yellow leaves drifting down on a light wind, and there was a promise of sunset.

As Mervyn reached the house that Sylvia and **Rodney** had shown him that morning, the front door opened and a posse of small children poured down the steps to be claimed by waiting escorts. A young woman came last holding by the hand a small boy in a red anorak and a woollen cap with a red tassel. She saw Mervyn, and asked him if he was the friend who was coming for Guy Landon.

"Yes, I am. Hallo Guy."

Guy did not answer. His teacher, who thought that Mervyn looked rather scatty, said, "Guy, you won't forget to hold your friend's hand when you go across the street?"

Guy and Mervyn walked off together. As they reached the crossing Mervyn grasped the bunch of woollen fingers. Guy made no objection, but withdrew his hand when they stepped on to the opposite pavement. They walked on for a minute or two in silence, which Mervyn found embarrassing. Didn't children chatter? Why didn't the stupid kid say something? He supposed that *he* should.

"Did you have a nice day at school, Guy?"

There was no answer, Mervyn felt that the brat was defying him.

"Did you hear me, Guy? I asked you whether you had a nice day at school?"

"Yes."

"What did you learn today?"

"I didn't learn anything."

"But isn't that what you go there for?"

"No, we sing and draw pictures."

"But isn't that learning?"

This was not the kind of question that appeared to Guy to need an answer. Mervyn thought, "the child's half-witted". A minute later Guy asked,

"Why are you making that big hole at the bottom of the garden?"

"Who told you that I am?"

"I've seen it."

106

"You shouldn't be playing about down at the bottom of the garden. It's too wet."

Nancy sent me out by myself one day because she wanted to write a letter."

"Why couldn't she write it with you there?"

"She said I made too much noise. There are steps in the hole, aren't there? Is it going to be a house?"

Mervyn had an inspiration.

"No. One day it's going to be a swimming pool."

"I could help you dig it. I've got a spade."

"You couldn't dig that heavy soil."

"My spade is metal, not wood. Can I go down the steps?"

"No. Not until they are finished. But then," Mervyn improvised wildly, "you can learn to swim in it."

"Will it be finished soon?"

"No, it will be a very long time."

Guy said in a resigned voice: "It would be quicker if I helped you."

They had turned into Robin Hill. A neat dark blue van was coming up the road towards them. "That's the laundry." Guy said.

The van stopped half-way between the convent gates, and the gates of Hollycroft. A young nun in a black caped coat with a hood pushed back from her face, jumped down and slid a letter into the bright red pillar-box which stood out sharply against the evergreens and leafless trees. The nun skipped quickly back into the van which drove off.

"I could have posted that for her," Guy said regretfully.

"You couldn't reach the opening."

"I could if you lifted me up."

"Well, we aren't going to post any letters now. Come along, hurry up, let's get in out of the cold."

24

Rosa woke before the light came. She noted with relief
that she was still alive, and began to take stock of her bodily
sensations. The pain in her back was acute, but that would
decrease when she was up and had begun to move about. The
pain and stiffness in her left leg might get better or worse as
the day went on, according to whether she managed not to jar
it, or to the weather or to some inexplicable programme of its
own. She felt a heaviness in her head, to which she was pretty
well accustomed, but the stickiness and soreness of her eyes
could be dealt with, and she knew that after washing she
would feel fresher and less tired.

What a bother, what a humiliating bother it was to have to
think first of these things on waking. How different from the
mornings when she had awakened full of coiled energy,
already singing in her head the songs that she would be
singing in the opera house or in the concert hall that evening!
Or those other mornings when she would awake with the
Italian sunlight on the walls of her room, when she would pull
on a housecoat, and run down the garden to lean over the old
wall where lizards flicked and capers grew in the cracks, and
from where she could see the towers of Florence catching the
early light. Well it was all the past now, the colours paler, the
feelings historic. What was vivid was the struggling remnant
of life and the fear of death, sometimes taking different forms,
this illness, that accident. To oppose it she had only the
remnants of that great power of enjoyment which made her
even now clutch at any fragment she could enjoy, like a child
clutching at every piece of furniture in the room when being
carried off to bed.

Anyhow this was Saturday morning, the best morning in
the week. The workmen paid or unpaid, were not there. Guy
did not go to school, there was often a chance of seeing him

about. Sylvia and Rodney were in and out. Dutton, if not in Bradford, could be heard telephoning from his room, visitors came to the house. Rosa felt much more part of an active world.

While she was dressing she heard the sound of the convent chapel bell, very clear this morning, the wind was blowing from the north. It was always a welcoming reminder to her of kindness within reach. Though she did not pray herself she found an irrational comfort in the knowledge that other people so near were praying.

While she was brushing out her hair, grey now, but once so thick and dark that it had been difficult to dispose of it all under a fair wig, she heard Guy singing on the landing below. It sounded like an attempt at one of the folk songs that he learned at his school. Quietly Rosa opened her flat door so as to hear the not very tuneful tones that still had a sound of happiness. He was not allowed to make a noise on the landing, if anybody happened to notice him, and in a minute or two the door of the flat below opened and he was called inside. Rosa, smiling, began to make her coffee, and carried it back to bed.

The morning was fine and dry with a pale blue sky and a sparkle of sunshine. Rosa decided to go for a short turn in the garden. Wrapped in her heavy fur-lined cloak, with a sequined scarf tied over her head, she made her laborious way downstairs, across the littered hall, and out of the front door.

The garden paths were not easy walking, they were still thick with clotted leaves, although Mervyn had been trying to clear them.

Rosa thought that he might be working in the garden. He was somebody to speak to, he always answered her politely; to exchange a few casual words with anybody was one of her small pleasures. This morning she could not see him anywhere about, but as she toiled down the central path Guy appeared from behind the tool-shed. He was wearing wellington boots, a padded coat and a woollen hat that was too big for him and tipped over his nose.

"Guy! Are you all alone in the garden."

"Mummy and Daddy have gone shopping. Mummy said to go and find Mervyn but he isn't here."

"Perhaps he has gone shopping too."

"Yes. I think I'll go in now."

"Would you like to have a short walk round with me first?"

"I'll show you the swimming-pool."

"Is there a swimming pool?"

"Yes, it's the one that Mervyn is digging."

It must be some game, she supposed.

"Do show it to me then."

"It's under the trees. It has a door over it sometimes, but he hasn't put it back."

She followed with difficulty in among the tree-trunks and the brambles. When she saw Mervyn's work, it seemed to her perfectly natural that any child should think that the hole was a swimming-pool, but rather odd that the young man who always looked as though any work with gardens was an unwelcome effort should have bothered to dig it.

"It's got steps down inside," Guy said.

"I see it has. But what are they for?"

"So that people can get further down to dig. I'm going to help him with my metal spade."

Rosa, who could not get right up to the edge of the hole because of a bramble bush, peered at it.

"Isn't it very deep, Guy? You must be careful not to fall in."

"I won't fall in."

Rosa shivered, "Shall we go into the house now, and we'll go up to my flat, and have some coffee together?"

One of Guy's favourite treats was a little cup of hot milk tinged with coffee. He turned with alacrity towards the house running ahead of her. Round the corner they met Mervyn, carrying a coil of rope. Guy ran to meet him.

"I showed Rosa your swimming-pool."

"I told you not to tell anyone about it! I told you it was a secret! I don't know what you're doing down here at all. You're a very naughty little boy, Guy. Go indoors at once."

"I am going."

Rosa interrupted, "You needn't speak to Guy like that Mr Ellis. And you need not be afraid that I should interfere with anything of yours. It's all I can do to get to the bottom of the garden."

He looked overcome.

"Oh, of course, I didn't mean to be rude. It's just that I didn't know that there was anybody down here, I didn't know that I was supposed to look after Guy except for fetching him from school. There isn't anything to see yet. It's only a bit of digging I've been doing just to clear out some of the branches. I was surprised to find anybody else in the garden. I do apologize."

"Whatever the hole is for do please take care that Guy doesn't fall into it."

"I will, of course I will. I shan't let him come down here at all."

"He *said* it was going to be a swimming-pool," Guy repeated as they walked slowly up the garden.

25

SUSAN AND RODNEY both complained at times of "the big shop" that they had to do on Saturday morning, but they really enjoyed it. They bought most of their food for the next week, filled up the gaps in their drink cupboard, and indulged themselves happily with small extravagences. Sometimes they took Guy with them, but it was much easier without him. Rodney always took back a toy for him or bought him some of the charming, bright sports clothes fashionable for little boys. He liked to see the child's face when he was pleased. He knew that it was the feeling of being tied to a permanent set-up which stood between him and Guy. He was not aware how much jealousy of Sylvia's love for the child came into it. He suspected that Sylvia wanted another one, and that would enclose him again in a world of perambulator and nappies, in which he had never felt at home.

This morning without Guy they got through quickly. They were having friends to dinner that evening. Sylvia loved doing this and was good at it, not only in the food she provided, but in a warm and lively welcome which made people like to come and see them. Rodney was pleased and proud that they liked coming.

They sat down to have a cup of coffee before loading their purchases on to the car. Feeling unusually benevolent, Rodney asked as he seldom did, "Where did you leave Guy?"

"In the garden. Mervyn is there working at his swimming-pool."

"How does he get on with Mervyn?"

Better than I expected. I don't think Mervyn and Guy actually like one another, but they don't seem to dislike one another. Mervyn bought Guy a packet of Smarties yesterday. Guy's very much interested in the swimming-pool."

"What swimming pool, for heaven's sake?"

"Well, you know or perhaps you don't, that Mervyn is making one at the bottom of the garden, he's cleared a space in that bit of wood, and he's digging a hollow for the pool."

"Nonsense, Syl, he can't be. He could never make a pool with a garden spade in that place among all the tree roots, and in that heavy soil. It must be a tale he's made up to amuse Guy."

"Mervyn hasn't got as far yet as making up tales to amuse Guy. He's been working on something down there for quite a time. Sam Dutton knows about it, though I don't think he's ever been to look at it. But he fancies the idea of a swimming-pool for his luxury flats."

"He must be mad. I'm not surprised at Mervyn, but I should have thought Dutton might have a little more sense. Have you seen this pool?"

"No. It's been such awful weather for going down that rough garden. And it's supposed to be a secret. Guy's the only person allowed to see it."

"Allowed or not I think we'd better have a look. If Ellis is digging fairly deep there will be water at the bottom of the hole, quite enough to drown a child if he fell in."

"Guy says Mervyn is making steps down the side."

"Tell Guy not to go near it again, until we give him permission, Sylvia! I don't know why we stay in this place!"

"Because it's roomy and we've made it comfortable and it's a reasonable distance from both our jobs, and the rent's so low it gives us a chance to save for a house."

"And are we?"

"Are we what?"

"Saving for a house."

"I've saved some, not so very much."

"Same here."

"The trouble is we like spending it."

"What's the use of saving a lot to get a house when everything's so impermanent? I think a flat such as we've got seems more appropriate than a house with these bombs going off everywhere. We can always keep on making plans for a house which does nearly as well. Meanwhile, after I've had a drink, I'll have a look at this swimming-pool while you get lunch ready."

"Bring Guy in, will you? He must be covered with mud by this time."

Sylvia vanished into the kitchen. She was not particularly worried about the swimming-pool. Mervyn seemed to her such a mild and harmless creature that he was not likely to do anything dangerous.

Rodney was not so sure, he had always thought that Ellis was a bit crackers. In an unusually parental mood he thought

113

that it might be all right to employ him as a companion for Guy for a few days, but Sylvia's habit of *laissez-faire* might be overdoing it this time. Why didn't she ask her doctors, who valued her highly, for an hour off, and slip round to the Registry? Rodney, usually prompt in action himself, liked other people to be. He poured himself a drink, and decided that in a few minutes he would go out and look at this swimming-pool nonsense, and perhaps tell Ellis it was out-of-bounds for Guy, and bring the kid in.

He was saved this trouble. As soon as he opened the door of their flat he saw Guy coming downstairs, from the second floor, a large peacock's feather in his hand, and an air of happy complacency on his face as of a guest well aware that he has given quite as much pleasure as he has received.

26

HER WALK DOWN the garden and Guy's visit had made the morning unusually stimulating for Rosa. She cooked herself a nicer lunch than usual, and after it had a pleasant sleep. When she woke, the sunlight had gone. It was only half past three but a darkening sky made it already begin to look like evening.

It was very quiet in the house: no builders; Guy, she knew, was going out with his parents in the car. She glanced out of her window before settling down to read, and saw Mervyn Ellis trudging down the garden path. He disappeared round the corner of the tool-shed.

What an odd young man he was; he couldn't really be trying to make a swimming-pool down there? That must have been a tale he told to Guy. But what was he doing? Why had he been so frightened and so angry when he found out that Guy had shown her the absurd hole? What was he digging it *for*?

She became uneasy, because of course the child would run

down there whenever he got the chance, it was the only thing in the neglected garden that could possibly interest him. Could Mervyn be hiding bombs down there? Or was it a grave? Had he murdered someone, and buried the body? She shook herself. All that was melodrama, the climate of opera, in which she had spent so much time for so many years. But what other climate did we live in nowadays?

Deeply disturbed she got up and began to move about the room, putting away some of the many things that always lay about there. Should she perhaps have a word with Guy's mother? Sylvia seemed to her a very affectionate, but slightly careless mother. Guy's father? She hardly knew him, and was not attracted by what she did know; he would think her fussy and interfering, and laugh at her. She had not seen anything of the family together, but Guy had unconsciously shown her that there was no very warm feeling between him and his father, who probably wouldn't look at the hole. She did not think he would bother to inquire what Mervyn was doing in the garden, and she knew that Mervyn's position in the house was uncertain. He was not likely to be the permanent caretaker, even if there was a permanent caretaker. Any suggestion of trouble about him and he would probably have to go.

Moving restlessly about her room, she came to her desk, and thought of letting the whole thing slide and sitting down to write one or two letters that she had put off for weeks.

As she looked down at her desk, she saw a piece of paper with handwriting and numbers on it. She could not remember what it was. She picked it up, and put on her reading glasses. It was the note of the telephone number at Blent Street Police Station; it was signed "Mary Copthorne, Detective Constable".

Rosa thought that she would have a word with the girl, ask her to come round for a cup of coffee, and perhaps mention the hole. She had, after all, been asked to mention anything unusual, and to mention it to a young woman, detective or not, seemed somehow less serious than mentioning it to a policeman. She picked up the receiver and dialled the number.

27

AS A RULE the bell of Mervyn's flat only rang when the milkman wanted to be paid. Surprised by it this afternoon he hastily collected some change and ran downstairs. He was startled to find on the threshold Inspector Corby, and a tall fair young man, not in uniform, but he looked like a policeman.

"I'm sorry to disturb you again, Mr Ellis. This is Detective Constable Trent. We want to have a look at the pit you are digging at the bottom of the garden."

"Oh, certainly, yes of course. Do you mind waiting while I put my boots on? It won't take me a minute. I'll just run up to my flat."

"That's all right. Detective Constable Trent will go up with you."

So they did suspect him of something! Well if it was still bombs they were after he had never had anything to do with them. He was the last person who would want to. He did not feel as secure as this ought to have made him. He prattled nervously as he ran upstairs.

"I'm sorry there are such a lot of stairs. I'm on the top floor. It's cheaper, of course, and you do get a better view."

Divided between a wish to conciliate the detectives by hurrying, and an opposing wish to annoy them by keeping them waiting, he pulled one long boot on an inch at a time, and then hastily crammed on the other one; the detective constable stood looking out of the window, and remarked,

"It's a big garden. Do you look after it all?"

"I just do what I can while I'm looking for another job."

116

Mervyn tugged a jersey over his head. "I'm ready now. Sorry to have kept you waiting."

The three of them went out of the house, and down the path towards the tool-shed.

"They'll feel bloody fools when they find nothing wrong," Mervyn said to himself, but he had an uneasy feeling that if they didn't they might invent something to justify wasting their time. He was sure he had heard of the police doing that. His mind had a way of picking up any bit of gossip or news that suggested a threat to the ordinary citizen.

Trent fetched a fork and spade out of the tool-shed, and went down the hole. He spoilt a good many hours' work, throwing up spade fulls of wet clay, and breaking down the steps which Mervyn had carefully supported with broken pieces of brick. No wonder they couldn't find any bombs or gelignite if they looked in such improbable places!

It seemed a long time before Trent finished, but he came out of the pit at last, glanced at Corby, and shook his head.

"There's nothing there, Mr Ellis," Corby said.

Mervyn thought "I hope you feel like the damned fools you are." He said, "Oh, but of course you have to make sure, don't you? One understands that."

"I want to talk to you Mr Ellis. Can we go up to your flat for a few minutes?"

Mervyn offered the detectives the two chairs and himself sat on the end of the bed, wondering what on earth the Detective Inspector wanted to talk to him about, and whether he should say that he wanted to have his solicitor there; but he had no solicitor, and did not know the name and address of one. And after all why should he need one? He was fortunately unaware how frightened and guilty he looked to Corby.

"Will you tell me what you are really digging that pit for?"

"Just for a bit of exercise. I like digging." Mervyn smiled uneasily. "It's good exercise in cold weather, it warms you up."

117

"From the look of the garden you could get all the digging exercise you want without making any more."

It seemed best not to answer.

"I believe you told the little boy who lives in this house that you were making a swimming-pool. But that was just a game, I expect. Did anyone ask you to do this?"

"No, but I suppose there's nothing wrong in digging where you like in the garden you're supposed to be looking after?"

"Nothing whatever, but you seem to have put a lot of work into this pit, constructing steps and so on. I think you must have had some purpose?"

There was silence.

"Come on now. If you don't tell me I shall have to ask you to come to the police station with me."

Mervyn, looking desperate, reached under the bed, and pulled out a shabby, old despatch case. He opened it and extracted a catalogue illustrated by coloured photographs.

"There you are if you must know. That's all I'm doing. I want . . . I must have a nuclear shelter of my own." He crouched on the bed and covered his face with his hands.

Corby turned over the pages.

"I see, but why shouldn't you have one?" Mervyn spoke from between his fingers. "I'm ashamed of being more frightened than other people."

"We're all frightened really. We all know we're living on the slope of a volcano. . . . I'm afraid even children know it. I think we all wish there was something practical we could do, but when people who have the most power don't really seem to know what to do, so many of us just feel helpless. But you're trying to save yourself, anyhow. Only, do you think you could ever dig a large enough pit to hold one of these?"

"Not the big sizes that have water storage and heating, even a sort of cooking stove. I couldn't ever manage that, and they're frightfully expensive. I could never save up enough to buy one. But if you turn to the back page you'll see there's quite a small one. It's rather like a tin drum, and you put a

118

certain amount of earth on top of it, as much as it can support. And it says you could live in it for seventy-two hours."

And what would you find, Corby wondered, when you came out?

"Mr Ellis, have you got a good doctor?"

"I haven't got a doctor. I haven't been ill since I've been grown up."

"Why don't you get on to the list of one, and tell him how you feel and ask him to put you in touch with a psychiatrist, at one of the hospitals perhaps. He or she might be able to help you."

"How could any psychiatrist alter the world?"

"He couldn't, but perhaps he might be able to help you to live in it as it is."

"I don't see how."

"You could try it. Remember there is always the possibility that those in power may realize just as the rest of us do that nothing could come of a nuclear war but entire destruction. Don't you think so?"

"No. I expect they want to destroy themselves and other people. Everyone feels like that sometimes."

"Everyone feels like doing a murder sometimes, but most poeple don't do it."

"More and more of them do. It only needs one or two people to destroy us all."

Corby looked thoughtfully at the tormented face: "Have you a family?"

"My mother and father are both still alive."

"Do they live in London?"

"They live in Lincolnshire. I haven't seen them for more than two years."

"Don't you get on with them?"

"I do with my mother. My father despises me. I hate him."

"If you saw him again you might feel differently, and find that he was very glad to see you. Anyhow I think a change

119

would be a good thing. I must go now. Will you remember to get in touch with us if you notice anything odd going on here or anywhere else? And if you decide not to go on preparing for the shelter, it would be better to fill in the pit. I don't suppose that many people go down here, but a child might fall in. Or the people who live in the housing estate beyond could get over the wall—and put their rubbish down there. I should finish with it if I were you.

Mervyn had only just gone back into his room when there was a loud knock on his door.

"Oh, come in."

Dutton came. "What were the police doing here?"

"They wanted to look at that place where I'm digging at the bottom of the garden . . . in the wood?"

"What on earth are you doing that for?"

"I told you I planned one day to make a swimming-pool there."

"Yes you did now I come to think of it, but you don't suppose I took that nonsense seriously. What were you really doing?"

Mervyn had an inspiration, "I wanted to plant a tree, a sapling."

"Aren't there enough trees here already? You've had the job of sweeping up the leaves: I should have thought you would know that."

Mervyn was irritated into saying. "Yes, I have swept up as many of the leaves as I could, and I've done quite a lot of work in the garden since July. I haven't kept an exact account of the hours I've worked but I've done some nearly every day."

Dutton hardly seemed to be listening. "What did the police expect to find down there?"

"I suppose explosives for making an IRA bomb. That's what they're looking for, isn't it? But they've gone away now. Of course they didn't find any."

"I should hope not. And you, just don't dig anything else

there. I don't want the police hanging round any house that belongs to me. Do you understand?"

"Yes".

"Just get on with the other work."

Mervyn surprised himself by saying. "You were going to pay me for it."

Yes, I know I was. But I'm not very flush at the moment."

"You promised that I should be the caretaker and have this flat rent free. Perhaps I could have that now if you don't want to pay me."

Dutton stared in astonishment. What on earth was the matter with this lad, who always seemed so obliging.

"I can't make any arrangments like that till the whole house is finished. Then we'll see. You just forget all that nonsense about swimming-baths and trees, and get on with the garden, and you won't lose by it in the end."

Mervyn looked sulky but did not answer. Dutton was leaving the room but he paused in the doorway and fished out his wallet.

"Here, I'm not a hard man. I don't want you to feel you're getting a raw deal, so I'll give you something on account. I'm going out to meet a chap now. I'm late, I must hurry. Goodbye my boy."

He went downstairs quickly. Mervyn looked at the five pound note in his hand. Not being the kind of young man to laugh or swear or pursue Dutton he stood and listened to his footsteps receding.

Having been paid by Sylvia that morning for fetching Guy, he had shopped more lavishly than usual for the weekend. There were several things that he liked waiting to be cooked, but now he did not want them. He felt as if he'd been shaken, and did not quite know where he was after it. His secret was no longer a secret, and although the Inspector had not criticized his project nor laughed at it, Mervyn had understood that he did not think it would be much good. Easily dashed by what other people thought, he had lost a purpose that had sustained him. But he was too tired to think about it now, he was exhausted as if all his strength had been drawn. He threw himself on the bed, and almost before he could pull the rather meagre duvet right over him he fell into a drowning sleep.

When he woke it was dark. The duvet had slipped half off him, and he felt as if an icy chill was driving into him from his skin to his heart. He stumbled off the bed, switched on his electric stove, went to the window, and began petulantly to tug at the curtains.

Outside there was a wind blowing. The trees in the garden and in the wood at the end were tossing and straining. In winter you could just see through the wood behind the toolshed a few of the scattered lights in the housing estate beyond. It seemed to Mervyn as though this evening there was another light in the wood, a moving light such as somebody using a small torch might make if exploring the ground. After a minute he couldn't see it, and did not give it another thought. He pulled his thickest jersey over his head and went into the kitchen to cook himself a large, hot meal.

28

"*You're going to* drive this morning, are you?" Toby, settling into the driving seat, did not answer except by clipping his seat-belt.

"Where do you want to go, Shelton?"

"It's a question of where you want to go first. Are you going to the London Library this morning?"

"Yes, for a bit anyhow."

"Right. I'll drop you there and then take the car on."

"On to where?"

Shelton's eyelids flickered. "I'm not sure yet."

"You're always so mysterious. Will you pick me up at the library at three-thirty?"

"Are you going to be in the library all that time?"

"I don't want to be mysterious, but like you I'm not sure yet. I was thinking that it was an easy place for you to stop and wait for me a few minutes if necessary."

"Four-thirty would suit me better."

"Look here, I don't want to hang about in town all day every day."

"All right. All right. Split the difference. Make it four o'clock."

They were waiting at the bottom of Robin Hill. The traffic lights went green and the car shot forward.

"Before we separate, Shelton, I'd rather like to have a talk with you about one or two things. Let's go and have a coffee somewhere. I can't really talk while I'm driving through this sort of traffic."

"All right; stop for coffee wherever you like."

Shelton speculated uneasily on what the talk was to be about. Was Toby getting fed up with the present arrangement by which he and his mother contributed the largest share of the household expenses, and he had the minimum use of his own car? He had always seemed so obliging, so easy to handle. Of course they could not go on in this way for ever, Shelton had never expected it and would not even want it. The Greenways estabishment, though infinitely preferable to that awful overcrowded squat in Ireton Road, was not nearly good enough, but at the moment it must do. Shelton reckoned he would need Toby and his supportive mother for at least another year. By that time if he had managed to get a few more people, and a bit of capital into his private business he should be able to get a decent flat and a more comfortable way of living.

He glanced sideways at Toby's face, there was a frown on it but that was probably because he was concentrating on driving, of which, Shelton had to admit, he had done very little lately. It was the most damnable nuisance if Toby was going to get difficult just now when Shelton wanted to use all his own wits for handling Dutton. Two problems about

Dutton exercised his mind. Had Dutton really got any money or could he lay hands on any? He talked big, he talked plenty, but even if he could induce his wife to sell her house, and reinvest her capital, what would that amount to? Would she let Sam have a free hand with the proceeds? She seemed to be pretty firm with him.

There was a second and more subtle problem. How far was Dutton particular about the kind of business he invested in? It seemed to Shelton that it had been a mug's game to buy those two big, run-down houses which of course cost far more to convert into flats than Dutton had realized they would, but there was nothing illegal about the transaction. Dutton might be risking bankruptcy, but not prison or a fine. How much would it be safe to tell him? How much would it be impossible not to tell him? Did all his moral talk about what people ought and ought not to do mean anything, or was it a habit, a cover-up? Shelton sighed deeply, and almost wished himself back in the Ireton Road Squat, where at least there were people who talked straight, and knew what they wanted, and were out to get it.

Nor was Dutton his only worry. Larry, whom he had met in the Ireton Road Squat, was excellent. His technical know-how, and the speed and skill with which he worked made the whole enterprise possible, and if it was to expand they would have to find another one like him, which wouldn't be easy. But Larry had one fault, he went on a blind at the local pub about once in every three weeks. It did not seem to make any difference to his work, he reeled back to the yard and one, or if necessary two cars were ready next morning. Larry was a taciturn fellow when sober, but was he on these festive evenings when Shelton was not there to keep an eye on him? Well, it was a risk that had to be taken. Shelton turned his attention to Toby again.

"Let's go in here for coffee, Shelton. I can park outside."

Shelton pulled himself together. He would settle Toby first and then have further talks with Dutton, and try to feel his way further in. The café was almost empty. They collected two nasty-looking cups of coffee from the dejected boy behind the machine and carried them to a table on the other side of the room. Shelton smiled, pushed the sugar across, offered his packet of cigarettes. Toby, who seldom smoked, took one.

"Are you going to show me your new poem, Toby? I should like to see it."

"You will see it when it's printed, which will be at the beginning of next February."

"But we may not be able to bring out a number of the magazine by then."

"It is going to appear in a magazine called *Early Affirmations*. You probably don't know it."

Neither did anyone else except Toby's friend, the editor, and a few people who had rashly subscribed to the venture, but Shelton was startled. Printing Toby's poems in *Explosion* was, he knew very well, not only his hold on Toby, and his claim to the use of his car, but the bait which impelled Toby's mother to sign cheques.

"If this is a particularly good poem, you might have kept it for the next number of *Explosion*."

"When is the next number of *Explosion*?"

"As soon as we've paid their deposit to the printers, and got the material together."

"My mother sent the money for the deposit. I gave it to you."

"Yes. I know you did but I was short for the rent last time. You'd think that when Dutton can't afford to do anything to Greenways, and probably never will, he could have let us stay there rent free, '*permitted squatting*' I think is the right term for it."

"We can't expect everyone to do things for us for nothing."

"You're very cock-a-hoop this morning. I suppose you think you've written a fine poem. What is it about?"

"It's called 'Time Was but Will Time Be?' Something Truda said at breakfast one morning sparked it off."

"I must say I find it hard to believe that anything good could be sparked off by Truda."

"That's because you know nothing at all about poetry. If you had ever tried to write it you would understand that the spark may be anywhere. This is what keeps me hoping. I don't think by the way we treat Truda very well. We ought to pay her something."

"For sparking off your poems?"

Toby frowned. "Don't be a fool, for doing all the work of the house."

"Why should we pay her? She gets free board and lodging and a good home in easy-going company. She doesn't get ordered about by bossy women."

"She does by bossy men."

"I suppose you mean me?"

Toby, who did, was silent.

Things were not going well. Shelton forced himself to an effort.

"Toby, don't let's have a long argument about nothing. I'm very pleased your poem is going to be printed. It's just that I'm disappointed we're not going to have it in *Explosion*. But I'm sure you've got plenty of other good poems ready. Tell your mother we've had a run of bad luck lately, and ask her for just enough to pay the printers' deposit. We'll bring out a special number with several of your poems and a note about you, and a photograph. And if we can spare it we'll give Truda a pound or two at Christmas. Now let's get on. I'll take you to the library, and I'll fetch you from there or from anywhere you like at three-thirty prompt. Okay?"

There were several things that Toby would have liked to say. He would have liked to know where Shelton took his car off to every day. He would have liked to go too, or to have the car all day himself sometimes. He did not want to ask his mother for any more money. He would have liked to ask why Shelton contributed so little himself. He would have liked, though perhaps not quite so urgently, to pay Truda a small

126

wage, but he was not capable of a sustained burst of even mild aggression. He had gone as far as he could for one day.

'That's all right, Shelton. Take the car. I'll walk on from here to the library. Pick me up at four o'clock like we said. See you.''

For once leaving Shelton to pay for the coffee, he walked out.

29

MARY COPTHORNE WAS walking down Cheriton Street. She had been to see an old pensioner in the council estate who had complained to the police that two young men were planning to break into her house and murder her for her savings. They were always hanging round and peering in at her front window; once when she came back from shopping she had found them at the back of her house, looking in through the kitchen window. She was afraid to go out and leave the place, but she had to go to draw her pension and to buy food. If she saw the young men hanging round near her door as she came back, her legs trembled so that she could hardly walk home, and she could not sleep for thinking about them.

She had called at the police station to report all this. The two young men were not in sight when Mary visited her. Mrs Broughton had no telephone; she was not on very friendly terms with her neighbours. She liked, she said, to keep herself to herself. Both her neighbours had noisy, badly brought-up children, she did not want to have anything to do with them.

Mary suspected that she was a difficult old woman, and that the young men might be harmless. Mrs Broughton could be imagining the whole thing. The youths, probably, were more pitiable than threatening. But of course she might be right, they could be watching for an opportunity to rob her.

Mary examined the fastenings in the house, recommended

a chain on both the front and back doors, anti-burglar locks on the windows. Mrs Broughton grumbled about the expense of these devices and asked if the police would provide them. She refused to consider putting her savings in a bank or a Post Office account.

"I've got a good hiding place for them here," she said. "I shan't tell you where it is," she added, with a malicious gleam in her eye. "Tell one, tell all."

Mary could only repeat her advice about chains and locks, write down the address of a firm in Cheriton Street who supplied them, and promise to come again soon when the young men might be about. She tried to call at the two nearest houses to ask if anybody had seen the youths but nobody was at home. She left feeling as often happened when she had answered an appeal for help that she had done no good.

She was troubled about her quarrel with Robert. Sometimes she said to herself that it could not really be a quarrel, they would both have forgotten about it by next time she saw him. But she did not take steps to see him. She picked up her telephone once or twice and then put it down again. He did not ring.

The celebration evening had made it impossible to postpone or dodge the situation between them. He had asked her to marry him; she didn't want to, she was happy with things as they were; he wasn't, she could no longer postpone seeing that; she was angry with him, but she certainly did not want to lose him. She thought he was old-fashioned and selfish. Young in some ways for her twenty-eight years she saw him as a character in *her* story, she could not see herself at all as a character in his, and she was angry with him because he did.

She was sick of worrying about the whole thing, but her training, which she had thoroughly and eagerly absorbed, made her always observant above her own preoccupations. As she walked down Cheriton Street she saw ahead of her an odd little figure, a short girl wrapped in a sort of rug, and trailing two plastic shopping bags so full that they almost touched the ground. Of course! It was the orphaned-looking girl who lived with the two men in Greenways.

Truda turned into the only café in the street. On an impulse Mary followed her. It was an unattractive place smelling of stale food. On the counter under a smeared glass cover were sandwiches wrapped in cellophane, and a chocolate cake trimmed with yellowish mock cream that looked as though it had been permanently waved. There was hardly anyone in the café. Truda sat down at an empty table, lowered her heavy bags to the floor and with obvious relief flexed her arms.

Mary crossed to Truda's table and put her hand on the back of a chair.

"Do you mind if I sit here."

Truda said "No" automatically, but looked doubtfully at the intruder.

"Why, we've met before," Mary said. "I came to your house the other evening with the Inspector."

"Yes. I remember now. You're police."

A girl leaning sleepily against the counter came over to them. They ordered coffee, and Truda said in a voice that sounded defiant "I'll have a piece of that chocolate cake." She would have liked to move to another table but she did not know how to do it. May looked at the bags of shopping.

"You have a lot to carry, haven't you? Will you be able to manage all that back to Greenways?

"I always do."

"Don't they take you shopping in the car sometimes? Do you drive yourself?"

"I don't know how. Anyhow they would want the car, they go out in it most days."

"To work, do they?"

"No. They work on the magazine at home. But they always go out. Toby goes to libraries, to read books, and he tries to get his poems published."

"Does he? And the other one? Shelton Gaines, isn't that his name? What does he do?"

"I don't know what he does." Truda hated to admit this. It made it seem as though she was so entirely outside Shelton's confidence, as indeed she was.

She added, "Toby doesn't know either".

"It's Shelton's car, is it?"

"No, it's Toby's."

The girl brought their coffee and Truda's cake. Truda wriggled in her chair. She wanted Mary to go away and leave her to enjoy her treat alone. But Mary felt that she was on the track of something odd that might be interesting.

"I used to make chocolate cake sometimes."

"Don't you now?"

She felt a pain as she remembered making one for Robert. But that would surely soon come right.

"Did you find the job at Greenways through the Job Centre."

"No." Although she only half-trusted this policewoman, Truda was so entirely unused to anybody finding her interesting, that she could not resist answering. The unwanted child of a brief affair, she had been dragged up by her unwilling mother until she was ten, when her mother went off with another man and Truda was taken into care by the council. Care was safe, there was enough to eat, and it was warm enough, they tried to be kind, but she had an unshaped longing for something more personal.

"I was working at The Three Feathers for a bit while someone else was in hospital. One of the things I did was at lunch, when people came in for snacks, I used to clear the dirty plates off the tables, and I got talking to Shelton and Toby, and they asked if I wanted a job in a house where I could live. I knew I couldn't stay at The Feathers after the other woman came out of hospital, so I went to Greenways."

She put the last fragment of cake into her mouth, and wiped her lips with the back of her hand.

"Have you found out who wrote that letter, yet? The letter about the bombs?"

"The letter didn't actually say anything about bombs. It just said that something was going on at Hollycroft."

"Oh, well, I don't know anything about it. I've never been inside Hollycroft."

"If you happened to notice anything unusual going on in Greenways or Hollycroft, would you ring me up if I give you the number, and tell me about it?"

"I'd tell Shelton. He could ring you up if he wanted to."

That, Mary recognized, was all she was going to get, anyhow today. But she had something. She said goodbye and left. Once, as she walked down Cheriton Street, and looked back, she saw Truda trudging along, her two heavy bags of shopping dragging over the pavement.

Corby looked up from the thick pile of reports, the usual stories of futile visits to house after house in their district. He pulled a half-sheet of typing towards him.

"Sit down, Mary, and tell me about this. Where did you come across the girl?"

"I was walking down Cheriton Street, and I saw her in front of me loaded with shopping bags. She dived into a café, so I dived in after her."

"You say the two men go off nearly every morning in Forrester's car and come back late in the afternoon. But she has no idea where they go. She's sub, isn't she? It struck me she was."

"Yes, I think she is a little, but she's got a certain shrewdness too. She's wary. The two men just use her as a drudge, but she half-likes it. She was mostly brought up in care."

"So anything personal makes a change. Does she sleep with either of them?"

"I don't think so. I don't know if they sleep with each other; that may be why Toby is so docile. After all it's his car, and he

131

doesn't have the use of it for most of the day. According to Truda, he doesn't even know where Gaines goes in it."

"That may just mean that they don't tell her. Does Gaines go to any kind of work in it I wonder?"

"They're all on social security."

"So it would be a dead secret if he did work."

"Did you know that he was in The Feathers the night the bomb went off?"

"Yes, I saw his name on the list."

"He was with Dutton, at one of the tables. Toby Forrester was alone at a stool at the bar."

"So Dutton and Gaines were having a private conversation."

"If they knew anything about a bomb in the car they wouldn't have been likely to be in The Feathers. Except of course that they wouldn't be expecting it to go off there. Anyhow it would be perfectly natural for Dutton to be having a drink with his tenant in the nearest pub. But why leave Forrester out of it? Those two houses and that letter about Hollycroft stick in my mind somehow. I think we'll follow Shelton to wherever he goes one morning. I'll put Chris Trent on to it, he can follow them in a plain car. Thank you, Mary, I think you've probably done a good job. You'd better come back when I see Chris and brief him."

As she rose Corby noticed her unusually slow and languid movements, she looked pale and heavy-eyed.

"Anything the matter? Are you well?"

"I'm all right. I've got a headache, that's all."

You haven't been quarrelling with you boy-friend, have you?" He was surprised by the effect of his casual remark. She whisked out of his room, and shut the door with something like a bang.

She has, Corby reflected. They'll get over it, I suppose they'd better, though I don't want to lose her from the Force, and I've never thought him good enough for her. Perhaps she's through with him. It would have surprised him to recognize that he found the idea cheering.

30

CHRISTOPHER TRENT DREW up the plain police car on Robin Hill halfway between the gates of Hollycroft and the gates of Greenways. At this time in the morning the road was a river of traffic heading for the City or for Central London. Trent concentrated his attention on the entrance to Greenways, looking for the Ford Escort, which according to his instructions should emerge at about half past nine.

A Jaguar slid out from Hollycroft, and turned up the hill. Trent caught a glimpse of a man and a woman in the front seat, and of a child's face pressed against the back window. He had been carefully briefed about the inhabitants of the two houses; those would be Grainger and Landon taking their little boy to school before going on to work themselves.

A few minutes later the convent laundry van, looking—as always—freshly cleaned, passed him, and went on to the lights at the bottom of the hill.

During the next quarter of an hour no vehicle came out from any of the three houses. Trent waited with growing impatience. He had been promoted to the CID five years before Mary Copthorne. He liked the detective work better than ordinary police work, but found that it needed just as much patience and he was not patient by nature; he did not have Mary's feeling that the whole thing was intensely interesting, and might become more so at any moment.

He had often thought lately of leaving the Force, and getting another job, but what other job? He was thirty-three, he had a wife and two small children. Even if he could have borne the prospect of job-hunting for months, for a year or more, perhaps before he found one, he could not risk it for them. Sometimes he felt as if the whole thing, police work, wife, family had all happened to him without his own volition. And so probably it would go on while he rose slowly in the Force, while his amusing little children became tiresome teenagers, and his marriage became a habit which might or might not last.

The search for IRA bombs round London had at first seemed to offer new hope—perhaps a quick step forward in promotion—but as time went on and in their district they found nothing, he got more and more fed up with it.

He liked Corby, and on the whole liked working under him, he was so fair and kind, though tough enough when necessary, but Trent was beginning to wonder sometimes if his methods were getting a bit out-of-date, and whether his often brilliant hunches might become more of a hindrance than a help. He had got a thing now about these Robin Hill houses, just because of one anonymous letter, and a few hints of IRA presence in the neighbourhood. As if they hadn't had dozens of anonymous letters since the hunt started, and if the bombers had ever been in this neighbourhood they would have moved out at top speed after the premature explosion outside The Feathers.

No, there was nothing on Robin Hill, but a parcel of nuns, and one of the many developers who had bitten off more than they could chew. It was just that Corby had let his imagination rip. Oh, well. . . . He was, Trent believed, being considered for promotion somewhere, he had been off lately for several half-days without giving any explanation to his juniors. Probably he had been for interviews. And if Corby moved on there was only Marsden, getting nearer to retirement age, who had been in the Blent Street CID longer than Trent himself.

A Ford Escort swept out of the gates of Greenways, and turned downhill. It was the right colour, it had the right number, but there was only one young man in it. Trent had been told that there would probably be a passenger, the real owner of the car, for the first part of the journey. However this was evidently the car, and perhaps the passenger had over-slept. Trent held back as the lights went red at the bottom of the hill, and then followed the Ford at a reasonable distance up Cheriton Street. He was eager now; a chase was always intersting. He skilfully kept the Ford in sight while never coming too near it. The young man driving the Ford was a good driver; the pursuit needed all Trent's concentration.

Turning out of Cheriton Street on the crest of a slope, they both passed the Answold Comprehensive and the Wagon Works, then a couple of streets of small detached houses. Trent was beginning to wonder if his quarry was going to lead him outside the Blent Street district, when the Escort slowed down into one of those innumerable High Streets which divide London into so many urban villages. It was like all the others—Post Office, two supermarkets, a garage, three High Street banks, two greengrocers, a baker's, a hardware shop etc. The pavements were full with early morning shoppers, but there was much less traffic in the road. Trent had to leave more space between himself and the Ford; he hung on persistently.

The Ford turned into a narrow road that passed the end of a school playground. It was a dejected looking street, Trent thought, gaps between the houses as if some of them had been pulled down; a few tatty shops, that looked as if they were generally shut; the Ford drove round the end of the row, Trent followed cautiously. The Ford stopped outside a big gate set in a high wall.

Trent drove slowly, cursing because if he too stopped he might very well make himself conspicuous. In his mirror he saw the driver get out of his car, leaving it unlocked. He took a key out of his pocket and unlocked the gates. Trent dared not hang about too long, but there was a turning just ahead of him. He drove round it, jumped out of his car and ran back to the corner. He was in time to see the tail of the Escort vanishing through the gates which were at once slammed behind it.

He walked back past the gates. Above them he could see the upper half of a rather dilapidated little house, which was evidently inhabited for at the only window visible above the high wall there were curtains, and a kettle and a half-filled milk bottle were visible on the window-ledge inside.

There was an advertisement painted across the gates at the back

> T. Hewitson,
> Plumbing and Emergency Repairs,
> Removals,
> Small Van for Hire.

This inscription had evidently been painted some time ago. What had once been white paint was now yellow with whole letters missing here and there. Quite a few tiles were missing from the front roof of the house. In one place a gutter had broken, and a strip of it full of dead leaves hung down.

Trent walked round to the front of the houses, past a pub, and saw that the road was called Back School Lane. A tree which he had noticed from behind gave him the position of the house that had swallowed up his quarry. No. 17 boasted a shop window filled with a heap of junk, obviously just dumped there. It was the kind of shop window at which his wife liked to look, hoping to find a pretty plate or a small useful jug. She hardly ever did and this jumble of unmatched cups and saucers, tattered, second-hand paperbacks, and hideous, faked Oriental vases would not have tempted even her optimistic spirit. One yellowing card announced AN-TIQUES. The other, handprinted on a postcard, said "Shop closed".

Chris Trent rang the bell. In a minute or two he heard footsteps and the door opened. The driver of the car stood in the doorway.

"The shop's shut. Didn't you see the notice?"

"Yes, but what I saw first was the notice on the gates at the back about removals and a van for hire. I wondered if by any

136

chance you might be wanting a driver. I've got a clean licence, and I'm willing to work any hours. I'm out of a job, and I'm married, with kids.''

The light eyes were moving suspiciously up and down him. Chris Trent wished he did not remember his mother-in-law's remark when he was promoted to the CID, that, uniform or not, anybody could tell that he was a policeman.

''The people who had the van have left. There are no jobs here. Try the Job Centre.''

The door slammed. Trent went back to his car and drove to the garage in the High Street. Things were going his way, it was a Heron Garage. He asked for an oil change; a young man came out to give it to him.

''Do you know a house, No. 17, Back School Lane, where there's some sort of yard behind, and there is a notice chalked up on the gates that they've got a removing van for hire?''

''There were some people that lived there three, four years ago; they had a little van and they brought it in here once or twice. I'd just come here then, but they left soon after. I don't know who lives there now, nor whether they've got a van or a car. They don't use our garage.''

''Is there another one?''

''Anderson's down the road, below the caff. I don't know who goes there nor anything about them.''

Trent had the impression that he did not want to know; probably there was no love lost between rival garages.

He drove to Anderson's. There seemed to be no one on duty; the place was shut, perhaps for the midday break. He could see a biggish yard, and at one side of it two or three cars for sale with price labels on them. He was ready for a midday break himself, he drove back to the pub, which was beginning to fill up. He got himself a pint of beer and a sandwich, which he carried to a table near the door, already partly occupied. Here he got a bit of luck. Shelton Gaines came in, another young man with him. They walked quickly past Trent to the bar.

There was a discarded newspaper on one of the chairs at Trent's table. He picked it up and screened himself with it. There was no reason why Gaines should be surprised to see in the nearest pub a young man who had called at his house . . . if it was his house . . . to ask for a job. But the less he saw or knew of a detective who was tailing him the better. Gaines and his companion hoisted themselves on to bar stools; Gaines was wearing a thick windcheater over the suit in which he had come to the door, but the other young man was in denims and a sweater, both stained all over with paint. He had a flop of hair which fell over one eye and shook as he gestured; he seemed to be angry.

They stayed there long enough for Trent to have eaten half a dozen sandwiches, if he had had them, but at last they slid off their stools, and turned to come down the saloon. Trent raised his newspaper, and did not risk looking up.

They were anyhow too much absorbed in each other to notice other people.

"Don't you bloody well forget," the young man said, "that I take the first risk."

They pushed out through the swing door. Chris Trent thought he had earned another drink and went to get one.

31

CORBY REPLACED THE receiver.

"The anti-Terrorist people have nothing under sus in West Walburn . . . haven't heard of 17, Back School Lane. Did you find out who the house belongs to?"

"Yes, the Council. They bought the whole of that strip of land for the education people in '76, when there was a plan to pull down the playground wall, and the houses beyond, and to enlarge the playground, which they say is not big enough for the number of children. They were also going to build two new classrooms. The whole thing had to be dropped of course

. . . no money, new projects cut, and at present not much hope of any extensions to the school grounds. So they pulled down one or two of the most dilapidated houses in Back School Lane and let the others when they could for what they could get, and did the absolute minimum, of repairs on them.

"No. 17 had been occupied for a few years by the man who had the van I heard about. Then it was empty for a bit; about six months ago it was let to a man called Larry Hawkins. He said he was a joiner and a plumber and was going to do odd jobs. He told them the roof was leaking, which didn't surprise them, but he hadn't mentioned it again, so they concluded he must have done an odd job on it himself. They really haven't bothered about Back School Lane at all, though I daresay they would if money began to flow again."

"It's Larry who pays the rent." Mary Copthorne observed, "But I suppose Gaines supplies the cash, out of Forrester's mother's contributions. Gaines keeps himself well in the background."

"It's a good hiding hole," Trent said eagerly, "because no one would think of there being one so near a school."

"They'd forget that a school is only alive in the daytime."

"It's in the day-time that Gaines goes up there."

"Tony Forrester really might jib if Gaines took his car out every night."

"You'll go in?" Trent demanded.

"Yes we'll go in. One day when we know for certain that Gaines is there. You'll have to follow him again Chris, and radio back to us, and we'll come. I'll bring three men up with me and join you."

"With guns."

"Yes I suppose so. If the IRA really are there they'll have them."

"You don't believe they are, do you, Sir?"

"It doesn't smell quite right to me. But I've no doubt that there's something going on there, and we'd better see what it is."

139

A minute or two after Trent and Mary had gone out, Corby was summoned to Etheridge. He had begun to like him better with only occasional lapses into his first dislike. Etheridge treated him well, was friendly, and always complimentary about his work. The lapses into dislike were in the moments when Corby felt that this genial behaviour was dictated by policy rather than by genuine friendliness. And now Etheridge was putting the idea of promotion before him, no doubt with a mixture of both motives. The idea was so new that Corby had not yet even mentioned it at home, because he wanted to make his own decision first. It was a good job, head of station on the outskirts of North London which carried with it the management of four sub-stations.

Anyhow Etheridge had put his name forward and wanted to tell him that it was on the short list, so as he came back to his room he knew that he must now consult Lucy. They had quarrelled furiously the night before. It was Tilly, of course. He had accused Lucy of being spiteful to her and Lucy had replied, "You've always been half in love with her". The constant friction between mother and daughter was making home miserable for them all. He was so fond of them he ought to be able to get them out of it.

He would take Lucy out to dinner that night. They had been economizing on treats lately, saving up for Christmas when Mike and Jessica would be at home too.

It was not Lucy's voice that came over the line.

"Tilly! You've got home from school early, haven't you?"

"I haven't been at all today."

"Why not? Aren't you well?"

"I felt sick this morning."

"I hope you feel better now."

"In a way I do. But I feel so sick every day at the thought of school that I don't know how to bear it."

"It's not long to the Christmas holidays."

"I feel it's longer than I can live through."

"I think you'll survive. In the meantime is your mother in?"

"No. She's still out at her computer nonsense."

"When she does come in, will you ask her to ring me up?"

"If I remember."

"Please oblige me by remembering. Goodbye."

His telephone rang as soon as he put the receiver back.

"The Mother Superior of the St Aloysius Convent wants to speak to you, Sir."

"Put her through."

The voice that came over the line was elderly and had a faint foreign accent.

"Inspector Corby? I understand that you are head of the detectives."

"At the Blent Street Station. Yes Madame."

"One of your officers came here a little time ago to make inquiries as to whether anything unusual had been seen here. I thought perhaps I should let you know that one of our Sisters, Sister Veronica, has reported to me that she has seen a young man once or twice, 'skulking' in the wood at the end of the garden."

"Can she describe him at all?"

"No. I asked her. She only knew that he was dressed in dark trousers and a jersey. I must explain to you that she has been very ill, and is only just allowed out. The doctor has advised that whenever the weather permits she should take a short walk in the garden in the middle of the day. I think I should also tell you that she is old, and that during her illness she had a good many delusions. Our Sister Catherine, a young sister who is our regular gardener, and spends a good deal of time working in the garden, has not seen anyone at all in the wood."

"I noticed that the wall that divides all three gardens from the Answold Housing Estate is broken down in several places."

"That is so, and from time to time we have boys coming

over after chestnuts, or children to pick bluebells. But that is different. They are not attempting to hide and they jump back over the wall when we clap our hands at them. If Sister Veronica is right this young man seems to be looking for something."

"Please ring me at once if anyone sees him again. I suppose the Convent is locked up at night?"

"Certainly. We have patent locks on all the doors, and our nuns take it in turns for a week to see that they are all fastened. They know that I often inspect them myself."

"This would not be the young man who does some work in the garden of Hollycroft?"

"Oh, no, we all know him by sight."

"Thank you for letting me know, Madame. I will keep it in mind; will you be so kind as to ring me at once if the young man is seen again."

He sat thinking for a minute and then rang and asked for Mary Copthorne.

"You went a short time ago, didn't you, to see a pensioner on the Answold Estate who complained that youths were hanging about her house, and were probably planning to murder her for her savings. Have you seen her again?"

"Yes. I had to go to a house in the estate not far from hers where a woman had an accident. I looked in on Mrs Broughton on my way back here. She said rather reluctantly that the youths seemed to have moved away to another part of the estate."

"She's at the end near the Robin Hill Houses, isn't she? Do you think she would report to us if she saw any young men getting over the wall into their garden?"

Mary grinned. "I shouldn't think she would oblige us or anybody else if she could help it, but I'll try."

As she went out of the room Corby thought.

"She's one of the people I should be sorry to leave. She's going to be a first-rate police-woman if she sticks to it. Well, I haven't left yet."

32

IN ANSWOLD COMPREHENSIVE the school-bell rang for the mid-morning break. Tilly Corby's form thankfully shut away their notebooks and slammed down the lids of their desks. Miss Appleyard, who had been taking them for geography, held up her hand as the first of them rushed to the door.

"One minute. There is a message for you all from the Headmaster. School will finish this afternoon at half past three instead of four. There will be no rehearsals of form plays, and you will be glad to hear, no detention. There is to be a meeting in the Wagon Works up the road to decide whether there will be a strike there or not. The police expect a demonstration outside the Wagon Works. Dr Carleton wants you all to get away as quickly as possible. Yes, Tilly?"

"There ought to be a demonstration. I'm going to join it."

All those members of the Answold staff who had anything to do with her had agreed that the less notice taken of Tilly Corby's own demonstrations the better.

"Hurry up all of you and get back quickly. You know Monsieur Ballompré doesn't like it if you're not sitting at your desks when he comes in."

She knew really that it was no use saying this because none of them minded what M. Ballompré liked. Eager for the few minutes of chatter and unrestricted movement they pushed and jostled each other in the doorway. In the empty form room only Tilly was left standing up behind her desk.

"There *ought* to be a strike at the Wagon Works. That man ought not to have been sacked. It wasn't his fault that the machine was damaged. He said he hadn't had it thoroughly explained to him. He was only sacked because he is black. Those sort of things are always happening."

"It would be better to say, 'that sort of thing is always

happening'. It would be even better not to make assertions about things you don't understand. Its quite impossible for an outsider to judge without having any technical knowledge."

"I don't see why. It was fully explained on the radio this morning. I heard it while I was dressing."

Miss Appleyard had also dressed to the sound of the radio, but had not been sufficiently interested in the dispute at the Wagon Works to take in what was explained about it. She said with a forced smile and an attempt at lightness,

"I hope you will remember your geography as well as you remember what you heard on the radio."

"I shall. I always do."

This was undeniable. It was Miss Appleyard's first term at the Answold, but she already knew that you could not fault this exasperating child on her work.

Tilly put her head on one side, and opened her eyes wide, looking innocent and surprised.

"But, Miss Appleyard, don't you think this man ought to be reinstated if it wasn't his fault?"

"Tilly, go along at once and join the others."

In the staff-room, drinking a cup of coffee that was already half-cold, Miss Appleyard exclaimed, "They always used to say that vicars' children were the worst, but really nowadays vicars young enough to have children at school are so relaxed that I wonder if it should be policeman's children."

"What should be?" someone asked.

"Who are supposed to be the worst."

"It sounds as though you've just had a brush with Tilly Corby?"

"She gets under my skin, and I know I shouldn't let her, but it happens before I realize it's happening."

An older mistress who was due to retire at the end of the next summer term observed placidly, "It's only come on lately, and it's just one of those phases they get. It will wear off again. Tilly is such a nice bright child."

The crowd of boys and girls poured out of the school gates

at three-thirty and quickly began to disperse. It had been a fine day but bitterly cold, and now there was a strong wind blowing. Tilly hesitated for a minute. At home there would be tea, and perhaps what she liked best, a toasted bun. There would be a warm room in which to do her homework that she always rather enjoyed.

There was a rule, a new rule, that if she went to tea with a friend after school she should ask permission to ring up her own home and say where she was. Tilly resented this rule, partly because she felt that it made her seem babyish in the eyes of friends who had more casual parents, but still more because her father had made the rule, she knew, for her mother's sake. Mam had made such an awful fuss one evening when Tilly went home with a friend and stayed watching television until after seven. Tilly, who knew very well that she had always been Dad's favourite child, now felt that he had deserted her.

Anyhow this afternoon she was going to break the rule. She was going to join the demonstration, and not go home till it was over, and if they were angry with her so what? She began to walk up the hill towards the Wagon Works.

She had not gone far before she found herself part of a crowd that thickened every minute. Many of them were black, but there were quite a lot of young whites, and of people of other colours. Tilly felt excited, she felt herself taking part in a protest against Racialism. As she came opposite to the big gates of the Wagon Works, she saw that the yard inside was filling with men pouring out of the sheds. The road was now completely blocked by people milling around in front of the gates.

Without any conscious purpose Tilly attached herself to a black woman who carried a baby, and had a small boy trailing after her. The woman was heavily built, she thrust her way through the crowd, the child tagging behind her, wailing a little, as he got pushed and found it difficult to keep up. Tilly followed him. The woman hoisted herself on to a doorstep; Tilly thankfully skipped up after her. She ventured a remark. "We can see everything so much better from here." The woman looked at her but did not answer. She only spoke in her own language to the little boy, who had stopped wailing, now that he was partly protected from the crowd by the door behind him.

It was growing dark. Tilly saw the helmet of a policeman here and there among the crowd. She heard the sound of horses' hoofs; a party of mounted police were coming up the hill; they turned off into a side street and Tilly could no longer see them. She was angry that they were there and that the number of police among the crowd seemed to be growing. At the same time, though she would not have admitted it, their presence made her feel safer, as she had always felt when she was in bed at home in the dark, and heard her father's step on the landing.

She was on the upper doorstep of two, and although she was small for her age, this made it possible for her to see over the wall into the yard of the Wagon Works, where arc lights were now turned on to an improvised platform. Several men were standing on it, one of them was speaking through a megaphone. It was impossible to hear what he said, but as the wind carried the sounds towards where Tilly was standing she realized that he was angry. This pleased her. She often felt that there were so many things to be angry about, but not enough people were angry about them. To be reasonable and calm nowadays was simply pretending that people weren't like they really were, and that you didn't live in a cruel, furious, dangerous world.

It was now quite dark. The street was crammed with people and completely blocked to traffic. In the Wagon Works yard the speaker got down from the platform, and another one got up, whom the crowd there evidently approved, they shouted and waved their arms.

Tilly, excited, craned up trying to see and hear more. She

146

did not notice that the woman with the two children had got down from the step and disappeared into the crowd. When Tilly did notice that she had gone she felt for a moment alone, and frightened.

Some of the young men in the road began to climb the wall; the police pulled them down again. A few managed to get over, police vaulted after them and they were pulled back struggling. The crowd surged forward and then back. Tilly was hemmed in on her doorstep, but said to herself that it didn't matter, she wouldn't want to get out before the end of the demonstration, and then everyone would go.

She was, however, considerably startled by an explosion on the other side of the road; a minute later a sheet of flame went up. People near Tilly said with satisfaction that it was a police car, and she was suddenly struck by the thought that her father might be in it or in one like it, anywhere. She shivered in the cold wind. Perhaps after all she would like to go home soon, but if she stepped down off her doorstep she was afraid of being crushed if there was another sudden surge of the crowd.

She felt a hand touching her leg, and shrank away from it, but it was not after her, it was feeling for a milk bottle. An elbow swung back and caught the side of her cheek, hurting her sharply, so that tears started into her eyes. Bottles and other things, she could not see what, were flying across the road as the small party of mounted police rode up the middle. Half the crowd ran before them, but a good many of the others closed in behind them, so that there was much more room on the pavement. Tilly stepped down from her doorstep and began to walk quickly downhill, away from the Wagon Works, towards the school. She saw that the street on her right from which the mounted police had come was almost empty, and turned into it.

With a deep sense of relief she reckoned that if she followed it, it would take her to the upper half of Cheriton Street. There she would be not far from home, she knew the way

147

well. She began to walk briskly along it. She had had enough of demonstrations for one evening.

She was a little surprised that her street turned up instead of down but she knew that Cheriton was a long street and she was sure she would soon come to it. She didn't. There was another turning to the right; no sign of the turning to the left that she had expected. She was puzzled, she began to lose what sense of direction she still had left. She was in a fairly long street now which had terraced houses with very small front gardens. In several of the houses there were lights on, and in one or two the curtains were not drawn, the light streamed out and supplemented the street lamps. It was not in itself a frightening street, but because she did not know its name nor where it was leading to Tilly was rather scared, and stood still to think for a minute.

A bus swung round the corner into the street, a small queue was waiting at a stop about a hundred yards lower down. Here was salvation, this bus was probably going to Cheriton Street. Tilly ran to join the queue, but checked as she was just going to join it, and stopped as the bus swung in towards the pavement. This bus had a number she had never seen before. She stepped back to read the name on the front. It was strange to her. The bus started off before she could speak to the conductor, and sailed up the road. Tilly was lost, she was in a foreign country, she did not know where she was or how to get home.

A supply teacher, who had been standing in for a day at one of the schools near, saw under a street lamp a little girl apparently about twelve years old, who was clutching her school bag as if it was her only possession in the world, and whose face in the garish light of the lamp was white and strained. He stopped and said to her,

"Have you lost your way? Can I help you?" Tilly saw a bearded face and thick spectacles bending towards her.

The nervousness that had really been below the surface of her mind ever since she left the school gates flared up into panic. This was the danger against which she had often been warned, the strange man who spoke to you in the street, the Rapist, the Strangler, The Murderer! With an inarticulate cry she fled from him, running as she had never run before in her life, without the least idea where she was going. She dropped her school bag and did not know that she had, she tripped and nearly fell on her face. She crossed a side road and only just missed being run over by a car. She stumbled against a wall, and did not know at the time that she had grazed her knee and bruised her elbow. She ran until she was out of breath and had to stop, panting.

As she got her breath back and felt steadier she thought how silly she had been. She had only to find a telephone-box in working order, and ring up her home, Mum or Dad would come in the car and pick her up. Then she realized that she had lost her school bag, and her purse was in it. She did not know where she had dropped the bag, it was no use going back to look for it. If only a vacant taxi would appear she could take it and they would pay at home. But there were not so many taxis cruising about in this part of London.

What part exactly was it? She looked round and saw that she was in a housing estate, which somehow felt if it did not actually look familiar. It also looked unalarming. There were people walking about and lights on in most of the houses. She tried to see the name of the street she was in; while she was looking a woman pushing a shopping basket on a stick came along the pavement towards her. Tilly went to meet her.

"Please can you tell me where I am. I lost my way by taking a wrong turning."

"You're in the Answold Housing Estate."

"Oh! Then it's near the school."

"If you mean the Answold Comprehensive that's just up the road."

"I don't want it now. I mean I've come from there, and I've got lost trying to get home. Am I near Cheriton Street? My home is quite near there."

"You can get to Cheriton Street in a few minutes. Go straight down this street to the end of the estate, and then turn to the right, you'll see a wall and a lot of trees above it on your left, but just keep on walking till you come to the main road, and cross it and you'll be in the upper end of Cheriton Street."

"Oh thank you, thank you very much."

Tilly walked on feeling like somebody who was coming out of a bad dream.

At the end of the street she saw the high wall, and the trees above it, their branches groaning in the wind. She turned right, and saw ahead of her only a few hundred yards away cars and buses going up and down the main road.

There was a street lamp at the junction of the two roads, in the corner house the curtains had not been drawn; a family party with children were having tea round a table, and the lights from their window streamed across the road, and reached the opposite wall, which was broken down in one or two places.

Suddenly, a dark figure jumped down over a broken section of the wall, landed on a pile of fallen bricks, and let out a *screech*. He had been carrying a bag which had flown out of his hand. He went after it, limping a little and cursing, grabbed the bag and went up the road that Tilly had just come by. He must be a burglar, but anyhow she was getting nearer to the main road with every step, and leaving him behind. She crossed by the lights and found herself walking down Upper Cheriton Street.

Oh how beautiful Cheriton Street was, how beautiful! There were the two supermarkets brightly lit and full of late shoppers. There was the greengrocer kept by an Asian family, who never shut it till midnight. There was the launderette with the row of women reading magazines or gossiping while their sheets and towels whirled round in the machines. To her surprise she saw by the Post Office clock that it was only a quarter to six. She was tired out and her bruises hurt, but she was safe and in a few minutes she would be home.

A young woman with a full plastic bag came out of one of the supermarkets. She was wearing a thick grey tweed coat buttoned up to her chin, and a little peaked blue cap which hid most of her fair hair. She stopped in the bright light from the supermarket windows.

"Tilly! It is Tilly Corby, isn't it? You won't remember me, I'm Mary Copthorne, I'm in the CID under your father. I used to come to some of Jessica's parties. Are you on your way home from school?"

"Yes."

"You've had a knock on your face, haven't you? Did you get it playing games?"

"No. I had a fall."

Something about the child, as if she had been upset, struck Mary.

"I'll just walk to your door with you."

Tilly did not want her at all. She didn't remember her, she was too tired to talk, she was thinking that while she wouldn't so much mind owning up at home to the demonstration, she would feel silly having to say how she lost her school bag.

"I expect you've been out to tea on your way home, have you?"

How many more questions was this woman going to ask? Tilly, tired of answering them, proffered a piece of information that was not about herself.

"I've just seen a burglar."

"What? Where did you see him?"

"He jumped over the wall at the end of the housing estate."

"Do you mean he came from one of the gardens of the Robin Hill houses?"

"I don't know. There's a wall with some of it broken down. I thought he must be a burglar because he was in such a hurry."

"Which way did he go?"

"Up the road down the middle of the estate I think. I didn't

151

wait to see. He was carrying a bag."

"What sort of bag?"

Oh this woman! Tilly decided to say "I don't know" to this and to any other questions that she might ask, but Mary Copthorne stopped.

"I must go back into the Station for a few minutes. You're nearly home, you'll be quite all right from here, won't you?"

"Of course."

Mary Copthorne went off quickly, Tilly turned into Calthrop Gardens, and saw ahead of her, with great relief, and some slight apprehension, the lights above the doorway of her home.

PART FOUR

33

ROBERT PRENTICE SAT in his office dictating letters. His instructions were very clear and phrased with careful politeness, but he was working above a ground swell of anger and misery. When he was thinking about Mary anger was uppermost, when he was concentrating on his letters it was only present as a sour taste in his mouth and throat.

"Okay Samantha, let me have them before lunch. There aren't many."

When the girl had gone Robert began to try and work on a diagram to see why the machine which had lately been supplied to a customer in Harrow, was stalling.

"Prentice."

It was Shepperton in the doorway.

"Your new car has just been delivered. It's in the yard, come and have a look at it."

The new car, a Vauxhall Cavalier, was brown and burnished as a chestnut just out of its green case.

"There." Mr Shepperton, happy in the pleasure that he must be giving, patted the shining bonnet.

"Take care of her. But I know you will, you're a good steady driver."

Robert would have been inhuman not to be pleased, but his pleasure was tangled underneath with weeds of disappointment. What lovely times he and Mary could have had in this car! Mr Shepperton was shrewd as well as kind. He detected the half-forced note of pleasure and gratitude. He said to

155

himself as he went back into his office, "They all take everything for granted nowadays."

As Robert drove up the hill towards Harrow, and felt the ease and strength of the new car compared to the old one, he had moments of real if shadowed joy. The shadow never quite lifted. All the time she couldn't ever really have loved him. He had known that she was getting completely obsessed with this police nonsense, but girls did get silly about things; he had not expected it to last.

Of course she had been pleased with her promotion, you couldn't expect anyone not to be, but that was three months ago now! She ought to have settled down to being in the CID. She probably would have if she wasn't so keen on pleasing her father's friend; and so delighted when she had manged to do it. Well, Corby was about fifty, and if she had to be silly about somebody it had better be about somebody like that, a man in a senior job with a wife and nearly grown-up children. Only why did she need to bother about anybody's approval, when Robert himself thought such a lot of her? She would probably settle down in time. But until she did he was going to leave her alone and she could see how she liked it. He wasn't going to risk being turned down twice.

It was a relief to be welcomed by the customer in Harrow, who far from complaining because the new machine had gone wrong suspected that it was something that he had caused by not understanding it. Robert found out what the trouble was in the first five minutes, and explained clearly. He had a cup of tea, and a chat about last week's football with the Manager, and left saying cheerfully; "That's it then, everybody finds these new valves difficult at first. We did ourselves. I don't think you'll have any more trouble, but if you do, just give me a ring, and I'll nip over any time."

He had meant to drive back to London before the exodus of the rush hour started, but his visit had lasted longer than he meant it to, and the road was already full.

He felt in his pocket for his cigarettes, then remembered

that he had smoked his last after his sandwich and half-pint at lunch-time. He did not smoke a lot, he was keen on keeping fit, but he wanted one now.

In the High Street of the next of the town-villages that string along on they way to London he saw a tobacconist's and sweet-shop. He also saw in front of it two yellow lines that prohibited parking. In a mood for petty defiance, he said to himself that there were no other cars near the shop, and he wouldn't be more than a minute. He drew up, half on the yellow line half on the pavement, and jumped out of the car. The shop was full. Children had just come out of school. An old man and a young girl were serving the mob of youngsters, and trying at the same time to keep an eye on a few of the bigger boys who were strolling about at the back of the shop and fingering wrapped sweets.

One big boy who was edging along the side-counter picked up with assumed carelessness a bright box of liquorice allsorts.

A young police-woman came into the shop, saw the youth with the box in his hand and said with a smile, "Going to buy that today, are you, Bill?"

With a sulky mutter he edged himself in front of half a dozen little boys taking their time over the important choice.

The police-woman turned to Robert.

"Is that your car outside, Sir? The Vauxhall Cavalier?"

"Yes"

"Perhaps you didn't notice the yellow lines. Would you mind moving it just round the corner into Market Street."

She was not really like Mary except in having a rosy face under the white crowned hat, but he answered her crossly.

"'I'm going in a minute."

"Didn't you see the yellow lines?"

"Yes. I saw them."

"May I see your driving licence, please?"

She looked at it carefully and made a note of the number.

157

"Now will you move the car. Then you can come back and get what you want in here."

"I don't want anything in this place."

He flung out of the shop, threw himself into the car, and drove off.

The evening traffic coming up the hill had thickened. Robert turned off the main road into a parallel side street, lined with parked cars. He was driving too fast, but he knew it. In another half-minute he would have re-entered the controlled surface of his life again. Still inwardly raging he did not notice a small van which swung out suddenly into the road.

He jammed on his brakes, but it was a few seconds too late. There was a loud crash. Half the doors in the street opened, windows flew up. Somebody near Robert was groaning. He felt that he was trapped somewhere. A feeble attempt to move brought a tearing pain in his right leg, and a sense of utter disaster.

34

CORBY WOULD HAVE preferred to swoop on No. 17 Back School Lane in the early morning when the school was shut, and there were likely to be few people about, but it was necessary to go in when Gaines would be there. With Williams, Byeford and a young constable called Denton he started ten minutes after Trent, who was trailing Gaines again in a plain car. The police car stopped in the road which turned off from the High Street, and waited for Trent's message.

"Both there. Gaines has left his car in the road this time outside the yard gate. They're in the yard, I can hear their voices but not what they say. They've got running water. It sounds as though they might be cleaning a car. The water's running out under the gate."

"Right, we'll come. Where's your car?"

"At the corner of the road."

"We'll meet you there."

"I'm going in by the front door with the search warrant," Corby said. "Williams, come with me. You three get outside the yard gate, and stop anyone who tries to get away. If I call you get into the yard. But remember no shooting unless they're going to shoot. We shall be at the front door in five minutes. I'll call you when we're there."

Evidently no one had tried to arrange or dust the tatty collection of objects in the shop window. The notice saying, ANTIQUES had been removed; the *shop closed* notice was still there.

Corby knocked sharply. For a second the frayed curtain behind the dismal window display was pulled back an inch or two, and a segment of a face appeared. The curtain swung into place again, but the door was not opened. They heard footsteps and movement inside, then a shout from behind the house, then a shot.

"Stay here, Williams. Don't let anyone get away."

Corby ran round the side of the house, pushing through the remains of a lean-to shed which propped or was propped by a wall.

The yard gate was open. Gaines was on the ground squealing while Trent twisted his arm behind his back. The other two policemen were holding a thin, rat-faced young man who seemed to be covered with blood.

Corby said to Trent. "Let's get him up. Hold him." To the others. "What's happened?"

"It's not blood, Sir, it's paint. He was painting that car red, and when he tried to run he knocked over the paint, and slipped in it, and fell, and got it all over him."

"Who fired the shot?"

Trent said, "I fired into the lock to open the gate, Sir."

"He's broken my arm," Shelton Gaines wailed.

"No he hasn't. Take them both inside, into the kitchen, I

159

have a warrant, Mr Gaines, to search this house." He held it out to Shelton who seemed too frightened to look at it.

"Come with me, Trent, we'll start upstairs."

It took them some time, for although only one bedroom was furnished and that with very little furniture, there were loose floor-boards, an old-fashioned chimney, and holes in places where the plaster had dropped off the walls. They worked in silence. Trent knew that Corby was displeased with him, and thought, "You can't handle any criminal with kid gloves nowadays, they'd only get in first. Our lives are worth more than theirs."

They came down into the yard. There were two cars, from both of which the number plates had been removed. One had been freshly washed and was drying; the other, a black Peugeot, was half-covered with bright red paint. Corby pushed open the door of a cupboard at the back of the yard. It was full of cans of paint, in one corner were a pile of number plates, a jar full of paint-brushes, and a box of tools.

Corby refrained from saying, "There are your explosives." He saw that Trent was red in the face and that his collar looked a size too small for him.

"Come on, we'll take them back to the Station now. They must have a bent garage somewhere. Might be Anderson's. They probably have regulars who steal the cars for them, and bring them in after dark. The owners of these two will get theirs back, anyhow. We shall get the names of the car thieves, and the garage from these two men. They don't look tough. They didn't offer any resistance really, did they?"

"No". Trent said grudgingly. "But if you wait until they have. . . ."

"We've a lot of waiting to do. On the way back to the station we'd better pick up Forrester and the girl from Greenways. They may be perfectly innocent but we shall have to question them."

He glanced at Trent's discomforted face, and added: "This

160

was a sighting shot. If there are any bomb-makers on our patch, you'll probably find them."

35

FOR THE FIRST time in her life Mary Copthorne found it difficult to sleep. She and Robert had often dropped off easily, happy and satisfied, in her narrow, rather bumpy single bed.

Now she was restless, her body craving, her mind disturbed. She had never expected that the breach would be permanent, but she did nothing to put an end to it. Sometimes during the night she thought how silly it was; how easy it would be next morning to pick up the telephone and say something casual.

"Hallo, Robert. How about next Saturday night?" "Long time no see. Would you like to have supper here this evening?" Or, nearer to the centre, "Robbie, are you still angry with me? I do want to see you again."

But it was not so easy as it seemed. If he snubbed her she would be furious. She did not quite believe that he would snub her. If he responded cordially the whole thing would start all over again. She knew that she didn't want to marry him. She didn't want "a reasonable job with definite hours". It had always been the belief of an unexamined part of herself that one day she would have children. Of course she wanted them.

But did she? Did she want several years of feeding them, washing them, nursing them, completely tied to them? Of answering their often repeated questions instead of trying every week to solve half a dozen interesting new problems? She would hate to give up the idea of ever having children; she would hate to start it now.

Robert, she thought, would be an affectionate and reliable father. But could she bear to spend all her time with somebody so set in his own ideas? She would rather have

161

children with somebody like Frank Corby, who always saw other people's points of view. The thought of not working under him any longer made her feel hollow; that was something she didn't want to lose.

But neither did she want to lose Robert altogether. She knew that if she made the first move he would be glad, especially if she did it with the suggestion that it had been mostly her own fault. But it hadn't, it hadn't! She was not prepared for complete surrender.

When she heard of his accident she was shocked and distressed, her tenderness reviving. She telephoned the hospital, she rushed to buy an amusing Get Well card and to send flowers. But she did not go at once to see him. She was half-ashamed of a feeling that his accident made everything more difficult; she could almost be angry with him for it, and this made her feel guilty. She told herself how specially busy they were at the station, and threw herself with even more than her usual energy into her work. Saying to herself each day that of course she was going to the hospital tomorrow.

Carrying two paperback spy stories, and a packet of Robert's favourite chocolate, Mary Copthorne climbed the steps to Ward G.II and stood in the doorway looking along the double row of beds. She was a little late; most of the patients already had visitors. Halfway down the line she recognized the bright blue of Robert's pyjamas; he was sitting up in bed reading a newspaper; he looked up, smiled and waved to her.

Her feelings of shyness and guilt abated, she walked quickly towards him, bent down and kissed him. The smell and touch of his face revived some of the old familiarity. Ridiculous to feel shy of him, but she had been dreading this visit, and had postponed it longer than she decently could.

"Mary! Very good of you to come. Pull up a chair." She put her offerings down on the bed. She saw that on top of his locker he had flowers, sweets, magazines.

"I thought you'd like these."

162

Thanks very much. I was getting short of something to read. They bring a trolley round, but there wasn't anything much left that I wanted by the time it got to me."

"How are you? How is it going?"

"Very well, they say. You know the leg was broken in two places?"

"Yes. I've been telephoning, of course, to ask after you and the sister told me that. I am so sorry. Is it very painful?"

"Not now while I keep still. I should be out of here in about ten days on crutches."

"And your job,—When can you go back?"

"To the indoor office work, probably, when I get out. They've got a temporary driver. They've been very decent. Mr Shepperton came to see me."

"Oh, good."

The both fell silent. A pretty young black nurse came up, glanced at them and stopped by the bed. She patted the bright coloured paperbacks.

"There now, those will keep you quiet for a bit."

He smiled at her. "I am quiet."

"Yes, you're a good patient."

The nurse glanced at Mary, then back at Robert.

"There's nothing you want, is there?"

"No thank you, nothing that you can bring me."

"Be good, then." She went on to another bed.

"Found any bombs yet, Mary?"

"No, not in our district."

"Too clever for the police, are they?"

"It's a big job searching the whole of London."

"Well, there seem to be plenty of you now."

"And plenty for us to do."

He flicked over the pages of one of the paperbacks.

"Looks exciting."

"I hope it is."

She longed to break through the ice. She felt the hard edge of hostility under his assumed cheerfulness. She stammered:

163

"I'm so sorry."

"These things happen."

"I feel it was partly my fault."

He went red. "Don't be ridiculous. It was nothing whatever to do with you."

"It . . . I. . . ."

Footsteps were approaching the bed. A stout, smiling Pakistani mother carrying a plate with a lid on; a teenage boy with a bunch of anemones, and two small children, each with a flower out of the bunch in one hand. They were all smiling, all exuding sympathy and affection. Of course, the Patel's, Robert's Pakistani family. They clustered round him, the two little ones tried to climb on to the bed to kiss him. The woman took the lid off the plate she was carrying.

"Look. A little taste of what you like. It smells good, doesn't it? They will warm it up here. When my husband was in hospital I took him some nearly every day because he did not like the food they gave him, he likes only the dishes of our country. Sometimes he had to eat it cold which is not so good but I think they will warm it up for you."

The teenage boy shyly put a fancy bar of chocolate into Robert's hand. Mary got up.

"Have my chair, Mrs Patel. I must go now. I have to get back to the station."

"Oh, must you go?" Robert sounded perfunctory.

"Yes. I'm on duty at six. I'll come again."

He nodded, and she knew that she would not really want to. She walked away down the ward. From the doorway she looked back. She saw that Mrs Patel had poured her ample weight on to a chair, the teenage boy and the two small children were all encamped on the floor round Robert's bed. He was opening one of the packets of chocolate that she had brought. There was a lot of chatter and laughter.

No one was looking after Mary. She was carried down in the lift to the ground floor, where a café, a book-stall, and a number of people milling in and out made her feel as if she was passing through an exceptionally clean railway terminus.

She felt very sad, but she knew that it had been a relief as well as an irritation to see the Pakistanis arrive. Her spirits lifted as she thought of going back to the familiarity of the police station.

In the CID room, she found one of the other young women detectives typing a report, and Chris Trent studying a map. He looked up smiling.

"Hallo! Been to see your boy-friend? How is he?"

"Getting on very well, thanks. He'll soon be out of hospital, and able to do the office work of his job."

"Good! By the way, do you know the news here? We're not supposed to know it yet. But I've been doing a bit of detective work inside the station for a change."

"What news?"

"Our boss is going, Corby. He's got a very good job. Head of Parbeck Station just North of London, with three sub-stations under him. So he won't be a tec any more but just control them."

Mary felt as if the ground had opened under her feet. The other young woman detective looked at her quickly and then looked down at her work.

Mary heard her distant voice say calmly.

"Oh. How splendid for him." She tidied her papers on her table without knowing she was doing it.

"I'm off now. Good night."

When she had gone out, the other girl said.

"She fancied him, you know."

"Corby? I didn't know. She's got this boy-friend anyhow. I wonder?"

"What?"

"Whether they'll make old Marsden head of C.I. here for the couple of years he's got left."

36

"WELL, IF THERE'S no help for it we'd better set out on this expedition," Rodney said. "I didn't know you wanted a house at all. I thought you rather liked this half crazy set-up."

"I'm quite happy here. It isn't that I want a house, but I do very much want us to look at this one."

"Because it belongs to one of your precious doctors?"

"Yes. Because Parkes has been so kind telling the agents not to put it on the market until we'd had the first look at it."

"We've seen it. We've been to dinner there."

"Yes, but you don't really see a house for living in by just going to dinner there, do you?"

"By God, you do want it! It would be too big for us surely?"

"It's not big. They moved in there after the second daughter got married. It's only got one more bedroom than this flat."

And who, he wondered would have that bedroom? He uneasily imagined a four-square family in a four-square house.

"If we must make this expedition what are you going to do about Guy? Your marvellous new girl hasn't turned up?"

"She will. She promised. She was going to have a farewell lunch with her boy-friend before he went back to his oil-rig."

"She seems to have forgotten the promise. It's nearly half-past three now."

"But we did have that message from someone to say she was on her way?"

"On her way from where? She may have gone back to the oil-rig with him. If we must go we'd better start now."

Sylvia turned to Guy who was building a garage on the floor.

"We shall have to leave you, but Vallery will be here in a few minutes. You'll be all right just till she comes, won't you? Daddy wants to go back and look at a house."

"Like hell he does," Rodney muttered.

Guy looked up from the garage. "Take me too."

"Yes, Rod, why don't we?"

"Because I won't go if he does. You can't look at a house properly with a child trailing round all the time. You've got him accustomed to so much attention he's always tiresome if he isn't getting it."

"Probably takes after you."

Sylvia loosened the child's grasp on her trousers.

"Bye, darling, Vallery will be here in a few minutes. Ask her to give you your tea. You know where the new cake is."

The door slammed behind them, their footsteps clattered down the stairs. Guy sent a despairing cry of "Mummy" after her, but knew that it was no good wasting tears.

His farm was set out on a table, he had been playing with it all the morning. The cows were in the field, the two pigs had their snouts in the trough: the farmer and his wife were just coming out of the doorway of the farmhouse. Guy snatched them up and threw them down on the floor. He trod on them, he jumped up and down on them, crushing them under his stout sandals. He swept the farm-house, and all the animals off the table to the floor. Then he kicked his garage out of the way, and marched out of the room.

His bedroom looked over the garden. He went to the window and stared out. Already in a day that had never achieved much light it was beginning to get dark. He looked across at the tool-shed and the wood beyond it.

They had told him that there was not going to be a swimming-pool. There wasn't room for it there. Mervyn had gone away to visit his father and mother. When he came back he would fill in the hole. In the meantime, Guy was not to go near it, he might fall in. He knew that when it had been raining there was always some water at the bottom of the hole. He would like to see if there was now. He could not have explained that at the moment he would like to do anything he had been forbidden to do.

His stout woollen coat and tasselled cap lay on the floor. He shrugged himself into his coat and tugged the cap over his head, crookedly so that the tassel hung down over one ear. He knew that he ought to pull on his rubber-boots but that was hard work with no one to help him so he left them lying there and went downstairs.

On Saturday afternoon there were of course no workmen about. The front door of the house was shut. It needed a key to open it from outside but, as Guy knew, it could be opened from inside by turning the handle. It was a big handle, but he had opened it before with both hands; he managed to turn it. He hesitated for a minute on the doorstep, as the cold wind stiffened his cheeks and forehead. The door shut to behind him. He had not thought of putting on his woollen gloves. He stuffed his hands into his coat pockets, and stumped off down the path towards the wood.

37

Rosa Spinelli had been out shopping in a hired car that morning. A visiting friend had told her that her clothes were falling to pieces and smelled of moth-balls, she really ought to buy herself a new dress. This presented difficulties. She could not find in any of the half dozen shops she had managed to penetrate, a garment that resembled anything she had ever worn. It made her angry that neither in shape nor material were they worth a quarter of what she was expected to pay for them. She was exhausted by getting in and out of the car, and by being pushed about in the shops. In the end she grabbed the dress that she could most easily imagine wearing and came home.

After these exertions her siesta lasted longer than usual. When she woke it was already beginning to get dark, and she realized with pleasure that it would soon be time to go round to the convent. Vespers were half an hour earlier on Saturday evening.

She went to her window to see what the weather was doing. To her surprise she saw Guy walking alone down the garden path towards the tool-shed.

She had met Sylvia on the stairs that morning and had heard that the new girl was doing well, and was coming that afternoon to be with Guy while his parents went out. Where was she, then? Rosa guessed why the child, on his own, was going purposefully down that path. Of course he was making for Mervyn's hole. Rosa wondered whether that limp young man had filled it in or covered it properly before going away. Perhaps this new girl knew nothing at all about it, and had let Guy go out for a bit while she was getting his tea ready.

Rosa began to draw the curtains and then stopped. So, for a minute did her heart. She could see the bright tassel of Guy's cap in the wood. She saw too a circle of light moving over the lower branches of the trees. The circle rose and then sank. Rosa realized what it was. Someone holding a torch must be moving about in Mervyn's hole.

She had of course heard from Sister Clotilde about Sister Veronica's story of the young man seen skulking in the wood. Whatever he might be doing there he must be up to no good: Guy ought not to be alone with him. But there was she knew, nobody in the house but herself, and it would take her so long to get out of the house and right down the long garden.

She picked up the telephone. The piece of paper on which Mary Copthorne had written the number of the Blent Street Police Station always lay on top of any papers on her desk. She dialled it and to her relief was at once put through to the CID and heard Mary's voice.

"I thought I'd better ring you. There's somebody with a torch moving about in the wood at the bottom of the garden, and the little boy, Guy is there too, nobody else is with him."

"Is there anybody in the house? The boy's father?"

"No, they're out, and Mr Dutton is away. The girl supposed to be looking after Guy hasn't turned up. I'm going out to him."

"We'll come at once. Be careful."

Without waiting to pull a cloak round her Rosa made for the stairs. When she tried to go faster she began to stumble and nearly fell. With a great effort she controlled herself, and kept to a pace that she could manage. It took her a minute or two to open the front door, the handle slipped from her grasp, but she moved it in the end, got outside, and turned the corner of the house. Guy was not in sight, he must be hidden from her by the tool-shed. As she came near to it she called out:

"Guy. Guy!"

There was no answer, but she suddenly saw the flame-coloured tassel of his cap among the bushes. She called to him again, but either he did not hear, or he didn't want to obey. As she pushed into the wood, sticks cracked under her feet, branches clutched at her sleeves.

"Guy. Guy. It's too dark and cold. Come in with me."

He did not answer. He was near the edge of the hole. The torch light was still making a moving circle on the trees.

"Guy! Come away from the hole!"

"No. I want to see."

She managed to reach him, and caught hold of his arm. He jerked it away from her.

"No."

She heard somebody laugh. The torch, turned full on to her face, blinded her. Then the light shifted and she had a confused idea that she was looking into a gun. The whole thing had become a nightmare. Without any consciousness of what she was doing, she pushed the child behind her. It was only afterwards that she remembered the noise of the explosion, and she did not hear the young woman detective calling her name nor the sound of men crashing through the wood.

170

38

"I ASKED YOU to come and see me, Madame Spinelli, so that I could say goodbye to you."

"You are going away, Reverend Mother? For how long?"

"But for always." The brown face under the coif wrinkled into a smile. "You did not imagine, did you, that I could be left in charge of this house after what has happened here? After such a public scandal?"

"It was not your fault."

"Indeed it was my fault: *mea maxima culpa*. That one of the sisters under my care should have been plotting for some time against the law of the land? That she should have been so near to the verge of madness that she tried however ineptly to kill you or the child, or perhaps both? That she should have had a gun in her possession? You will know now that for some months she has been in touch with her younger brother who has been working here in London for the IRA in hiding with one or two others. You have heard that I am sure?"

"Yes. I know that they have all been arrested."

"I knew that Kathleen O'Shane . . . she is of course Sister Catherine no longer, was a passionate girl, that she had been deeply affected by the death of her elder brother. He was shot, while laying an ambush, by an English soldier. But I did not know that the poor girl was so near to madness, I did not know that she was hiding gelignite in the laundry cupboards, and taking it to her younger brother at his lodging. The police are still trying to find out how it reached her. They suspect it came in to us disguised as a box of soiled laundry. It seems that when I took her off the laundry she planned to use the pit the young man Ellis had dug in the wood as a hiding place—she believed that as the police had examined it and had found nothing there, nobody would come again. You can understand what a terrible shock this has been to our Order. I am no longer fit to be in charge of a House."

"But what will you do? Where will you go?"

"I am going to my own country, to France, to the house of our Order near Frejus. I shall be relieved of all responsibilities; although I hope that I may be allowed to help with some little duties, I shall have most of my time to devote to prayer and repentance. But I did not ask you to come here so that I should talk of my own affairs. You are recovered from the shock?"

"Thank you, yes. I am no more shaky than I was before."

"And the child is all right?"

Madame Spinelli smiled. "He has been begging for a gun."

"You have always told me of your constant fear of death. You must be glad that you have proved yourself stronger than the fear. When what seemed to be the moment came, you thought first of the child."

"I had no time to think."

"There are times when all thinking is below the surface but even so one does not move a finger without thought behind it."

Rosa broke out in a cry of grief.

"What shall I do now? It has meant so much to me coming here."

"I hope you will continue to come here. I have not yet been told who will be Mother Superior here, and perhaps an introduction from me if I were to leave one, would not be a good recommendation for you. But the chapel is open for Vespers to anyone who wishes to come."

"I have no faith."

"I think you have more than you know, or why should you come here at all?"

"To see you."

"I shall often remember you in my prayers. I hope you will occasionally write to me and tell me of yourself. At Christmas

I shall be allowed to send you a greeting. You will be staying in your flat where you are now?"

"I don't know where else to go."

"Your daughter in California?"

"No. She is very happy in a full life with her husband and children, and her oboe. She plays the oboe in a good orchestra. I will not add what might well be an unwelcome tension. She has never suggested it. I do not think I shall leave my flat. I have so many possessions there. They are all part of my life, my books, my discs, my pictures and photographs. I do not think I shall ever find the energy to move them."

"The little boy of whom you are so fond, he will be there."

"I think not. The whole thing has given his parents a distaste for the place. They talk of moving to the house they went to see that afternoon."

"So that you feel now you have nothing left. But perhaps if there is a void the faith you really so much want will fill it. And there will be other people coming to live in Hollycroft; you have a loving heart, you may find a friend among them. I cannot talk to you any more now. I fly to France the day after tomorrow and I have a lot to do."

Already there was somebody knocking at the door. Rosa picked up her stick, struggled out of her chair, and with a last look at the face she would never see again went quietly out of the room.

39

"MRS SAMUEL DUTTON from Bradford asking to see you, Sir."

"Oh! Will you send her in."

Sam Dutton's wife at first sight was a long rich fur-fabric coat, and a big round hat of the same material. Between the two Corby saw a pink powdery face with full, pendulous cheeks, and a firm chin. The frame of the wing-tipped spectacles was studied with brilliants; the eyes behind the glasses were also bright.

"Good afternoon, Mrs Dutton. Won't you sit down."

"I'll be glad to." The furry column subsided on to a chair. "It's an old-fashioned building, this. You need a lift."

"We've been needing one for some time. What can I do for you?"

"I've come to see you about my husband, Inspector. Have you arrested him?"

"Do you think there's any reason why we should have?"

"I hope not." Her voice more broadly Yorkshire than her husband's suggested to Corby whose grandmother came from Huddersfield, a comfortable home.

"You see, Inspector. I've been uneasy lately about what was going on down here. My husband's a good man, but he's always been one to get himself into a mess if there's any chance. He's too hopeful, you see; its his nature. He doesn't tell me much but I knew there'd be trouble as soon as I heard he'd let those squatters stay on in that other house, Greenways. Mind you, I think Sam's sorry he ever took on that house, he's had so much trouble with Hollycroft. I warned him, but he never listens to me until its too late."

"He hasn't been arrested for anything so far, Mrs Dutton."

"Thank Heaven for that, and he's me to thank for it because I wouldn't let him have any more money. I knew he had in mind to use it in some wild-cat scheme, though he didn't tell me what it was."

"I doubt if he really knew."

"That young man, Shelton Gaines, told him a pack of lies seemingly. Anyone could talk Sam into putting money into a Merry Go Round if he had it, and most likely no Merry Go Round there at all. Mind you, he wouldn't want to have anything to do with bombs; but he could get mixed up with them without knowing. I knew from his talk that there was something wrong going on here. That's why I wrote you that letter."

174

"What letter, Mrs Dutton?"

"You must have had it, haven't you? I didn't sign it of course and I had it posted in London by a friend. It was after you all put out a notice about reporting unusual behaviour. I wanted you to keep an eye on these houses. Didn't you get the letter?"

"We did indeed, and we spent a good deal of time trying to find out what it referred to. As a matter of fact it put us on to something else, so I suppose I can't blame you for trying to hoax the police."

"I just did it to save Sam. It's what I've had to do in one way or another for thirty-odd years. Well, I mustn't take up any more of your time. I'm going to stay the night at Hollycroft and see what the builders still have to do. I suppose I can get a taxi round the corner."

"The Station Sergeant downstairs will ring for one for you. Thank you for coming, Mrs Dutton. Don't write any more anonymous letters, and tell your husband to keep out of our way."

"I will that. Thank you Inspector. Goodbye."